THE
GREAT
GREEN TREE
and the
MAGICAL
LADDERS

STEPHEN KOZAN
illustrated by Tony Maulfair

READYAIMWRITE
PUBLISHING

READYAIMWRITE
PUBLISHING

The Great Green Tree And The Magical Ladders

Stephen Kozan
Illustrated by Tony Maulfair

www.stephenkozan.com

First U.S. Edition, 2016

ISBN 978-0-692-46864-7

Library of Congress Control Number 2016931565

Printed in the U.S.A.

Dedicated to
Rick Bent &
Dean Montgomery

The torch stays lit.

"I have always been delighted at the prospect of a new day, a fresh try, one more start, with perhaps a bit of magic waiting somewhere behind the morning."

-J.B. Priestley

CONTENTS

AUTHOR'S NOTE

Dear Readers,

    During the past year I embarked on a school visitation tour where I spoke to students about writing and illustrating, and why it was so important for them to express their creativity and imagination. After each presentation, I was asked many cool questions. Those questions ranged from what's your favorite food to what's your favorite book. But one of the most popular questions I received was *what inspired you?*

    The answer to that question is really quite simple. *It's life.*

    I observe and absorb so much of the life that surrounds me, it influences me to write my stories. Yes, I write fiction, but you'd be surprised by just how many stories can manifest from *real* life situations and *real* people.

    For example, take this book you're about to read. In the backyard of my home grows a lush, vibrant dogwood tree. It's not huge, but it's large enough to command attention. It's especially pretty when it's in bloom. One summer afternoon, my kids asked if I would build them a ladder so they could climb up and explore its branches.

    I did.

    They took turns ascending the ladder and poking around through the various limbs and leaves, and then laughed when they wondered how in the world they were going to get down. I also observed insects interacting with them and how quickly I realized that neither of them particularly like bugs.

    So the wheels began spinning in motion. I sat in a lawn

chair and thought about the various behaviors of my daughter and her specific ~~distaste~~ *hatred* for insects. I envisioned that my dogwood tree was magical and that it was infested with creatures of all shapes and sizes. I dreamed that they had a purpose and a world of their own: a teaching tree for kids who misbehave.

What if *my* daughter became the loose interpretation of what this tree was all about? What if *she* became the protagonist and the tree interacted with her? *Well*, you'll have to read about that to find out.

So while my kids played in the tree, I grabbed a notebook and my G-7 pilot pen and scribbled notes as fast as I could. My brain became almost *magical* as a truckload of ideas, thoughts and characters barreled through my mind at warp speed.

This innocent tree that had been growing in my backyard for the last ten years was becoming the inspiration for my next book. This book.

I implore you as a reader or a writer, to pay attention to the life around you. You'll never know when something so *real* can morph itself into something that becomes *unreal*.

Thank you for making me a part of your reading journey!

Now buckle your seatbelt, and let's find some magic.

THE GREAT GREEN TREE

and the

MAGICAL LADDERS

CHAPTER ONE
FAMILY MATTERS

The house phone rings at 4:08 p.m. on a school day. Shea stops playing her electric toy guitar and shoots a guilty glance at her mom who is standing in the hallway holding the cordless phone receiver. Shaking her head from side to side, her mom answers with a curious, "Hello?" Her responses are brief. She nods in silent acknowledgment of what's being said on the other end of the line while staring at Shea with a disappointed scowl.

The call ends abruptly.

"That's another one this week, Shea! Do you know what this one's about?" her mom asks.

"Yes—and so what," replies Shea. "I'll do it again!"

Tears well up in her mother's eyes. She throws the phone across the living room, smashing it into the front door. It falls to the floor in pieces. "What are we going to do with you!? I can't take it anymore. You need help! *We* need help. Ever since the incident with the centipedes last summer, you've changed!"

"I *hate* bugs! You know that," Shea yells. Arms outstretched, palms up, Shea shrugs her shoulders and marches outside to the backyard.

Shea is a problem child. She is 10 years old—the younger of the two children in her family. Since the centipede episode, Shea's behavior has gradually become a nuisance for the entire family. She gets into trouble in school and disrespects her parents' at home. She's mean to her older brother, Christopher, and she's been involved in several fights with kids at school—all of which, *she* started.

Her dad, John Stonebrook, is a hard working self-made man who owns a sign business. He is proud of both the business he's built and the family he helped to create. He loves his family, all the way down to the family dog, Dillon—a fawn colored Boxer with a broad white chest, classic black chops, and a dusting of white atop his snout, like snowflakes that never melt. John feels a great harmony between humans and animals—something Shea doesn't appreciate or care to understand. On many occasions, he has tried explaining to her the importance of having a healthy relationship with the animal kingdom.

"We help them, and they help us," he says.

But despite all of John's speeches and discussions on helping others, Shea doesn't care. She is in the business of looking out for herself. Generosity is stupid—her word. "Why would I want to give away *my* stuff?" she chirps.

None of the potential consequences have been motivating enough to adjust her attitude. In fact, every punishment seems to just make things worse. Last time her mother demanded that she do her chores, Shea threw all of Christopher's socks into the trash compactor. She lies about everything from chewing gum during class to not having homework when she really does. And she steals whenever possible. Her teacher's reading glasses are still buried deep in the plant pot at the back of the classroom. And just last week, Shea snatched pizza slices off three younger students' lunch trays and threw them into the trash with a wink and smirk. There is no denying it. Shea Stonebrook is a troublemaker.

Lucy Stonebrook, Shea's mom (who, in Shea's eyes, is her main adversary), works part time for an Internet company. Primarily, though, she is a stay-at-home caregiver to the kids. She is a loving mom—some might say to a fault. She's quick to forgive and is far too tolerant of bad behavior, particularly from Shea. To outsiders, Lucy couldn't be a better mom. She tackles issues with open arms and ears, free from judgment and willing to consider a variety of solutions. But Shea views her mom as overbearing and annoying. Clearly, none of this is the case, though. For any adult who has ever tried to help Shea, it is easy to see just how skewed her vision of her own family is, and in particular, her mother.

Outside, Shea sits on the patio, cross-legged, mumbling to herself about what took place inside the house. Throwing the phone was unusually violent for her mother and somewhat alarming in the moment. But Shea is already filing it away as a distant memory. It is May and hotter than usual for this time of year, which only adds to the tensions surrounding her. Overhead, circling a pot of overgrown yellow bell flowers on the second-floor wood deck, large striped bees chase one another. Their legs are fat and full of pollen. Below, tiny black ants are patrolling the ground beside Shea's crisscrossed feet. This angers her. She scowls and snarls, "I hate you all!"

The ants are beating a single file path towards the gigantic oak tree growing in the Stonebrook's backyard. The tree is enormous. In fact, many of the neighbors are jealous of the tree because it is so gorgeous and tall. It is lush, full of life, and bursting with foliage. It's the type of tree that when you look up you can't see the top. The tree is so massive it's a miracle that the roots have never damaged the house. Strangers comment on the tree every June when the family takes part in the annual neighborhood yard sale. Younger children seem particularly amazed at the sight of the tree. They tug on their parents' sleeves and point. John and Lucy often hear astonished young voices say, "Ma, look! Look at that tree up there!" Entire families huddle on the front walk—mouths so wide-open that horse flies use their tongues as landing-strips, much like helicopters setting down on an airfield.

No one really knows how long the tree has been there, but judging by the mammoth size, it is easily over 150 years old. Everyone in the Stonebrook family loves the tree. Well, all but one...

It's around 5:45 p.m. that same night when the phone rings once again. Lucy has just finished duct-taping the broken battery cover and answers—much to her delight, this isn't a phone call

implicating Shea in some wrongdoing. Rather, it's her friend, Jill. Her daughter, Peyton, wants Shea to come over and have a play-date. Jill tells Lucy how Peyton has been nagging her all afternoon about inviting Shea to visit. "She is so *borrrrred*," Jill says, imitating Peyton's desperation.

Unaware of the phone call, Shea is still outside sitting on the patio, sulking. She had said her peace to the bustling ants at her feet and buzzing bees overhead. Now she's thinking up her next mischievous venture. Anything that will make her family mad sounds like a good time to her.

Just as she finishes concocting a new wicked plan for mischief, the French doors open up to the patio, and her mom pops out. She asks Shea if she'd like to be dropped off at Peyton's house. Without hesitation, Shea rolls her eyes and mutters,

"Thank God."

Lucy ignores Shea's sarcastic tone, and tells Jill they'll be right over. Lucy thinks it's in everyone's best interest if Shea spends a few hours away from home so she and John can regroup and, hopefully, cooler parental heads will prevail. It will also give Lucy time to make some important calls.

Having reached their wits end, Shea's parents have planned the kid version of an intervention to help each other in finding ways to try and steer Shea in the right direction. However, for now, the kid version of the intervention has to *exclude* Shea. With help from Christopher and the kids' grandparents, Lee and Marie Smith, as well as Johanna Meyer, they form a round table discussion in the family's living room while Shea is at Peyton's house. Both sets of grandparents give accounts of what they witnessed while Shea had spent time with them. Lee, Shea's grampy, speaks up first, telling everyone he's seen her steal candy from a handicapped neighbor boy named Sam. This has happened on several occasions. Each time Shea is scolded and punished, but it never stops her from doing it again. She has also disrespected grampy and lied to him on multiple occasions. Before he can finish, Shea's grandma, Marie, chimes in and says that she has also been disrespected many times. In addition to stealing candy from the handicapped boy, Marie has caught Shea muttering mean words about the boy and trying to get other children to pick on him as well. Shea doesn't have any compassion or even tolerance for his differences. This bothers everyone sitting at the table because they had not raised her to be this way.

John reluctantly shares his experiences regarding his daughter. He is concerned about her tendency for jealousy. She seems especially angry about shared friendships with others. At times, while doing random yard work, he has overheard Shea talk about some of her friends in a bad way. It is clearly jealousy. On one occasion, John noticed Shea being so bossy with a certain friend it bordered on bullying. Unfortunately, this is happening at school too, with kids she doesn't even know as well. These situations are the reason for the phone calls that Shea's mom keeps receiving. It is very troubling for the family to know their once sweet girl is wreaking havoc in school and bullying other children.

Next to speak is Johanna, Shea's Omi (German for grandma). With a sad face, she looks defeated. She, too, has stories of Shea's misbehavior. She describes an afternoon at the mall when she and Shea were sitting in one of the benches outside a clothing store. An elderly man was shuffling along with his metal cane. The man sheepishly approached them, donating a smile and a nod with a barely audible, "How do you do." Shea had responded to the man's greeting by sticking her tongue out then flapping her lips together, making a wet, vibrating sound. "A raspberry," Johanna repeated with a sigh. "She raspberried that nice old man. I was so embarrassed. I hope he chalked it up as a kid being a kid as he continued on his way. Much to my regret, it was awful manners," whispers Johanna. She opens her mouth to continue, but Christopher jumps in this time.

"She's not responsible!" he barks. "She hardly does her chores, if at all." Pointing at his parents across the table, "And *you* guys allow it!"

Chris has finally had enough of his sister's antics and launches a merciless assault, including a near-endless list of bad behaviors. Hands above his head, he says, "I accidentally stepped on her new shoes once, and she has never accepted my apology. She's terrible at forgiveness!"

Dillon, their dog, is lying at John's feet—head on his paws—probably wishing he could reveal his own misgivings about her. No one has ever observed Shea mistreating Dillon, but at this point, they wouldn't put it past her.

The "intervention" lasts about 90 minutes. They all seem a bit relieved by the healing power of sympathy and a sound plan. John and Christopher stand up to stretch, letting out a disgruntled sigh. They give each other an exaggerated high five, both hoping to have accomplished something. Lee and Marie embrace Johanna offering reassurance that everything is going to work out fine.

Even Dillon looks excited about something, probably because he's expecting to receive one of the organic treats Omi keeps stashed in her purse for visits. He hops out from under John's feet. With his little stump wagging, he twirls in a circle then drops his two front paws down on the carpet, signaling that he wants to play with his squeaky ball.

Both sets of grandparents say their goodbyes for the evening and head out the front door.

Arms folded, leaning against the foyer wall, Lucy looks at John and says, "How do you think it's going over at Jill's house?"

Hesitant, John walks over to Lucy and wraps his arms around her. "I think she's going to be alright, Babe," he says. "Have faith that something's going to change her."

Lucy feels assured and comforted in John's arms, but she isn't totally convinced. "I'm praying for a miracle," Lucy says.

"I'll do the same," John replies.

Holding hands, they walk down the hall and into the kitchen to plan dinner.

Christopher makes his lazy way down the steps. Gripping the walls of the stairwell, he jumps down the last four steps and chimes in, "How 'bout pizza? Shea's not here, so she can't fling pepperoni at us."

"Pizza sounds greeeeaaat," says Lucy. "I do not feel like cooking."

John kisses Lucy on the cheek then snatches the menu for Pizza Crazy out of the junk drawer.

Lucy hands him the already dialed phone.

"Hello…yes, Pizza Crazy—I need an order for deliv—wait, can you hold for a second? I have another call coming in."

::click::

"Jill?" John asks.

"Yes, John, it's Jill. Is Lucy there?"

John is puzzled by her shortness, and hands the phone to Lucy.

"Hi, Jill—what's up?" Lucy asks.

There is a long pause on Jill's end. "It's your daughter." Jill is steaming mad and doesn't hold back. "You need to pick her up, she's out of control."

Lucy turns to John, giving him a thumb down signal while Jill rants in Lucy's ear. John shakes his head and rolls his eyes. Before Lucy can tell John the story, John interrupts and says, "I'll go get her."

Lucy apologizes profusely to Jill and tells her that John will be right over to pick up Shea. Lucy presses the off button on the phone and places it gently on the kitchen table.

Christopher sighs and says, "I guess we're not having pizza."

Twenty minutes after nine, John opens the front door with Shea trailing behind. Dillon barks and greets both at the door. John bends down to pet his beloved friend, while Shea walks by. Immediately, Lucy zeroes in on Shea and begins screaming. "What in the world is wrong with you!? Why would you do that to Jill?"

10

"What'd she do?" Chris asks.

Lucy shoots a glare at Chris and shouts, "I'm not discussing this with you right now. Shea, go to your room and shut the door! You're in for the rest of the night!"

Lucy races upstairs herself, runs into the bedroom crying, and slams the door behind her. John attempts to follow, but as he reaches the end of the hallway, she sobs and tells him to please leave her alone. "I love you. You're a great dad, and this isn't your fault. I just need to be alone right now." She continues through muffled sobs, though John can't understand most of it, and what he can make out seems a bit out of place for this type of situation. But he respects her request and gives her some time to herself.

In the bedroom, Lucy is face down on the bed, her head buried in her clasped hands. Her legs are outstretched straight as an arrow; she looks like a totem pole. Weeping, she can't stop mumbling incoherent questions—mostly concerning where she went wrong.

She is also praying.

"If you can hear me, please, *please* help. Help our family. Help our daughter act right. What is wrong with her? Why is she so defiant and disrespectful? Why doesn't she respect anyone? All she does is lie, and steal, and bully people. *I* need help. *We* need help. *She* needs help."

The rest of the house has fallen silent. For the first time in Lucy doesn't even know how long, everyone is home and the house is *actually* quiet. She continues to lie on the bed, face down, hands clasped. Silently praying, she is desperately looking for answers.

She wonders, who, if anyone, could help.

Saturday morning arrives. Weather outside is a balmy 80 degrees. The unusual May heat wave presses on. The house is bustling, despite the rough previous night for everyone. Coffee is brewing. Fresh bagels are warming in the toaster. John is sitting on the deck drinking his iced coffee, reading news stories from the football sports application he'd downloaded on his phone. Across town, Christopher is being dropped off by grandma and grampy at Brightbill Field for baseball practice.

Shea stumbles down the stairs around 11:30 a.m. and finds her mom shuffling between the toaster and coffee machine. Sleep had pressed a self-induced delete button in Shea's brain, wiping out all memory from the previous night. Lucy has nothing to say to her. She is still in her nightgown, and her hair has a serious case of bed head. For obvious reasons, the last thing Lucy cares about right now is her hair.

Shea looks outside the kitchen window and immediately notices what a fantastic day it is shaping up to be. An easterly breeze blows through the tops of the pine trees and enters the kitchen window. Bright sun has warmed the windowsill. It really is a gorgeous day. Showing no signs of remorse for the night before, Shea turns to her mom and asks, "Can I have a play da—"

"Please don't talk to me right now," interrupts her mom. "Go ask your father for whatever it is you want."

Shea mutters something under her breath and spins around on one heel. Her attention turns to the sliding door where her dad is sitting on the deck. She slowly slides the screen door open, tiptoeing towards his chair.

"Yes, Shea?" grumbles Dad.

"I was just wondering…would it be okay, since it's nice out, that I have some friends over to play today?"

Her dad replies, "Under the circumstances, I'd normally say no, but I think we all need to immerse ourselves in constructive activities while we let this situation settle down a bit. I suggest you stay away from your mother today and do your best to be good."

Shea nods, and slaps her dad on the back, as if to say thanks then runs into the backyard. She opens the turtle-shaped sandbox, rummages through the shed for some butterfly nets, pulls out some walkie-talkies, and puts on her gardening gloves. About an hour later, two cars pull up alongside the curb. It is Genevieve and Josselyn with their moms. The girls run up the grass embankment towards Shea. Both girls have their hands outstretched for a high-five, but instead of Shea slapping their hands, she slaps them on the forehead.

"Hey! What was that for?" snarls Gen.

"Oh, I was just kidding. *Geeeesh*—take a chill pill," barks Shea.

All three girls sit down in the grass next to the giant oak tree. They giggle as Shea explains that they are going to be butterfly hunters today. They're each given a walkie-talkie, oversized round net attached to a bamboo pole, and a large empty mayonnaise jar they're instructed to use for stockpiling the captured butterflies. Gen and Joss are super excited to search the yard as butterfly hunters. While the three of them are still sitting, they decide on code names for walkie-talkie communication during their expedition. Shea is called "Dragonfly," Gen is "Cannonball," and Joss is "Starbird."

"This. Is. *Awesome*," says Joss.

"Best. Day. *Ever*," shrieks Gen.

"Starbird, Cannonball—let's hunt!" cries Dragonfly.

Due to the humid, sunny day, there is an abundance of white butterflies erratically flapping about. This is great news for the girls. An hour or two passes as the girls run around the yard, into the neighbors' yards, and across the street, tracking down the cute, white butterflies.

It is late in the afternoon when they finally end their butterfly hunting expedition. All three girls have bounties. Their mayonnaise jars hold five to six butterflies each. Genevieve, Josselyn, and Shea are ecstatic. They sit back down by the oak tree and hold their jars up at eye level—to get a good view of the butterflies against the sunlight. Shea is sitting in the shadiest part of the tree shadow, so she has to stand up to see her bounty properly. Gen also stands up because she is having trouble with the shadows. Joss feels left out, so she, too, stands up. While holding their jars, the three girls let out a laugh and high-five each other in unison.

Just as they are ready to sit back down and talk about the hunt, Shea notices a dreadfully large beetle (or what she thinks is a beetle) walking at a snail's pace towards the base of the big oak tree. Shea turns to Gen and says, "Guys, do you see the *size* of that beetle? It's huge. Look, it's got horn-like things on its head. What do you think it is? I think it's a beetle. It's black and shiny like one."

"I don't know, but it's gross!" shrieks Josselyn, her face scrunched.

"Totally," Gen says. "I think you should stomp on it, Shea."

"Yeah, kill it!" says Joss. "Step on it—it's gonna bite us!"

Shea sticks her index finger into her mouth and starts biting her nail. She's thinking. Her two friends are jumping up and down, moving their mouths and pointing at the beetle. Everything seems to be moving in slow motion. The lone, black beetle is getting closer to the base of the tree, moving ever so slowly. Time feels like it is standing still for Shea. She picks up her right foot and holds it in the air, about two feet above the ground. Joss and Gen are yelling at the top of their lungs. "Squish it! Do it! Just squish it!"

STOMP.

A moment later, it's over. Shea lifts up her shoe, and underneath, the beetle is no more. In fact, you could no longer tell it ever *was* a beetle. She feels immediate accomplishment. Her friends high-five her and continue cheering. Shea puts her right hand in the air, points straight to the tree branches, and proclaims a name for herself. "Shea Stonebrook, the mighty beetle killer!"

As she watches over her fresh kill, little does *she* know, some *thing* is watching over *her*.

CHAPTER TWO

A VISIT FROM THE GRASS KINGDOM

Two cars pull back up to the curb alongside the house. Shea's dad peeks his head out from the kitchen window towards the children still playing near the big oak tree and says, "Girls, your Mothers are here—time to go."

Frustrated, they release a collective sigh of disappointment that the play-date is ending. Gen and Joss gather their things and ask Shea if they can borrow the butterfly nets until next time. Shea shakes her head yes, and the three girls smirk at each other, giggling. They high-five once again and say their goodbyes. Shea watches the two girls skip down the yard towards the curb and into the waiting arms of motherly hugs.

Must be nice, Shea thinks.

And the cars slowly drive away.

Shea turns back around toward the base of the tree, where

the beetle—or what's left of him—lies on the grass. Next to the remains are the walkie-talkies and the three mayonnaise jars—butterflies still wildly flapping inside. On the western side of the big tree, she can see the sun lowering toward the horizon. It is still quite warm out. Sweat beads are speckled across her forehead from running around for the last few hours. Droplets collect near her brows, soak in, and eventually slide down her cheek, falling from her chin. She can't believe that her play-date with the girls lasted almost all afternoon.

Her dad pokes his head out of the kitchen window again. Hands cupped to his mouth, he bellows, "Shea, dinner time—let's go. Wrap it up, girl."

"Okayyyyyyyy," she replies reluctantly. "Comingggggg."

Dad shuts the window.

"I'll bet my dinner's cold anyway," she whispers to herself. "They love to serve me cold dinner. I'm the evil one," she mumbles. "I might as well take my sweet time." Walking toward the shed, butterfly jar in hand, Shea passes by her old playhouse. It had felt like a castle when she was five-years-old. Now it's partially overtaken by the honeysuckle bush growing next to the big oak tree. With a snarl and scoff, she points to the playhouse and says, "No one plays with *you* anymore." She snickers, turns her head, and continues her trek to the shed. But before she can take two steps, a faint voice whispers her name. Followed by a louder hiss with elongated pronunciation, "*Sheeeeeeeeaaaaaa.*"

The wind picks up a bit, and branches of the honeysuckle bush slap against the roof of the playhouse.

"Who's there?" she asks, frantically searching in all directions.

"Come closer. Do you see me?" says the voice.

"No, I don't. And this isn't funny!" Shea spats. Looking up at the second story of the house, she checks to make sure that her brother, Christopher, isn't playing games with her from the bathroom window.

No one is in the window, and it's closed.

"Okay, fine—I'll come closer, but tell me who you are," Shea replies nervously.

"Do you see me *now*?" the mysterious voice asks.

A moment later, Shea responds, "I do!" A thousand thoughts race through her mind while she tries to process what she's seeing. Right in front of her on the edge of a honeysuckle branch is a spider, with errr…glasses? Her glance darts left then right again trying to determine whether anyone is watching. She's convinced it's some sort of prank. "What are you doing here?" she asks. "How can you *talk*? Is this even real!?"

Using one of his eight legs, the spider pushes his slippery glasses closer to his face, giving her a courtesy bow. "I'm Webster. Lead tour guide of the *Great Green Tree* and Ambassador of the Grass Kingdom."

"The what?" says Shea.

"Grass Kingdom. I'm the tour guide, and Ambassador. The Governing Council sent me. I'm here for you," quips Webster, who seems to be in a hurry.

Shea takes a long, hard look at Webster, studying everything about him. He is about an inch long and light brown with lighter stripes. Obscure, dark brown patterns are woven into his skin. Most pronounced, though, are his glasses. He has eight eyes, but he is wearing a pair of glasses—custom spectacles made to fit all eight eyes, of course. A strap made from leaf stem connects to the frame and hangs down around his neck, preventing the glasses from falling off his face. But every now and then they slide a bit, and one of his eight legs has to shove the glasses back up to his eyes.

"So you have eight eyes, but you wear glasses," Shea laughs. "That's weird."

"Ironic isn't it," replies Webster. "But I need them. They are special glasses that allow me to *see* inside of the Great Green Tree." Webster climbs up the shaft of the branch and rests on the edge of a honeysuckle flower so that he is eye-to-eye with Shea.

She is still bewildered by the encounter.

Webster clears his throat and begins to tell her why he's really there. "I was sent here by the Governing Council. They were alerted to the unnecessary death of Roland, the Rhinoceros Beetle. You killed him." Webster glances down at Roland's remains. "He has a family, you know. It's a very tragic loss for them, all because of you, Shea. The Governing Council is also aware of your behavior towards your family, friends, schoolmates, and your treatment of the animal world."

Shea tries to ask a question, but Webster continues.

"They're watchers—the Governing Council. They keep tabs on everything that goes on between the human and animal worlds. They step in when they're summoned by calls for help from humans or when a wrongdoing or unnecessary death takes place in the animal kingdom."

"But—" Shea interrupts.

Webster continues, "I'm here to show you what's been in your own backyard all of this time. This tree we're standing beside, it's a special tree. It's a *Great Green Tree*. And it's been here for many generations."

"That's nice, but who *is* this Governing Council? And what is *the Great Green Tree*?" she demands.

"It's a refuge—a teaching center. It's a magical place where creatures of all kinds come to flourish, and educate children like you on their wrongdoing. You need help, so here I am. I'm going to be your tour guide through the tree. I'm going to show you a world you never knew existed."

"And this Governing Council, who are they?" Shea asks.

Webster scratches his head, pushes his glasses up again and says, "Well, it's complicated. As I told you before, they're world watchers. They're spiritual beings that are neither human nor animal. They seek harmony and peace between the two worlds. When they see trouble, they intervene. They're the creators of the *Great Green Tree*, and there's many of them planted all over the world. The Governing Council appoints guides from the animal world to educate young humans like you on how to be a better person."

Shea looks up into the tree and points. "You mean up there?"

"Yes, up there. I can take you," Webster says.

Webster, with his neck outstretched, looks up at the tree and carries on. "Many of the creatures up there have a lot in common with you. Some of them made bad decisions in their lives and were sought after by the Governing Council. Once found, they were educated on how to become better individuals. Some had terrible things happen to them in their homelands. They were summoned to seek refuge here, and to live in harmony with the other members of the community."

Dusk blankets the waning sunlight in preparation for nightfall. The cool night air has dried the sweat on Shea's brow and she's breathing normally now. Shea can sense that one of her parents is about to yell a second call for her to come in for dinner. (There is no third call in the Stonebrook household.) She puts her hands on her waist and considers everything Webster has told her.

"You haven't really told me who *you* are," Shea says. "You know, my mom told me never to talk to strangers. I think you owe me that."

Webster removes a tiny handkerchief from under his belly, takes his glasses off then fogs the lenses with his breath. He begins polishing his glasses while talking. "I told you, I'm Webster. Some call me Webby or Little Webby. I live nearby—not too far from here. I'm a fifth generation tour guide for the *Great Green Tree*. We're everywhere...us grass spiders. And yes, we *all* have bad vision. My ancestors were appointed as lead tour guides for the *Great Green Tree* because of our ability to navigate the Grass Kingdom. We're fleet of foot with a keen sense of direction."

Shea drops her hands from her waist and points towards the Great Green Tree again. "So you don't live up there?" she asks.

"No," Webster says. "I've never—*we* have never lived up there," referring to his family. "The Governing Council needs us to guide tours, and those begin from below. I often wonder what it's like to live up there. I hear so many good things from all the folks who live in the tree. Webster breathes deep and exhales slowly. "Truth be told, Shea, this is my first job as a tour guide. *You're* my first student."

He finishes polishing his glasses and tucks the handkerchief back under his belly then readjusts the stems of his glasses on either side of his head, reconnecting the strap around his neck. "You know," he says. "The Governing Council sends guides like me around the world in search of children who misbehave like you. The fact that you were chosen means you're very special."

"I don't know what to say," Shea replies.

"Saying you'll go sounds like a good response." Webster winks four of his eight eyes.

She replies, "But how? My parents are going to know I'm missing. They'll probably call the police or something. What if I get hungry? I can't be gone for days or weeks. This all sounds so crazy!"

Webster shakes his head causing his glasses to tilt sideways. "No, not days or weeks. This tree is pure enchantment, Shea. The Governing Council equipped this tree with magical ladders that activate a time freeze. To you, it might seem like days or weeks while you're up there. But down here, the clock will only move about an hour."

Shea scrunches her brow in a puzzled expression and scratches the top of her head. "And these magical ladders you mentioned—"

Webster's eyes grow with excitement. "Yes!" he says. "The magical ladders are the most important tools for this adventure." Webster points to a white ladder that Shea's dad had built for her and Christopher, "Your dad didn't know it, but *this* ladder started it all. He built the ladder because you and your brother were so determined to climb the tree that it sparked an overwhelming curiosity in you. Before your behavior spun out of control, you were a vibrant, little adventure seeker. You see, we can't *force* you up the tree. You had to want it for yourself. And your dad wanted to help. Now that the ladder is here, you have a gateway to our realm."

Shea is still apprehensive and struggling to understand. "But what makes me so special?" she asks.

Webster pushes down his glasses, and rubs his eyes. "Look, I just need to bite you."

"Bite me!?" Shrieks Shea.

"Yes, I need to bite you. My venom is a shrivel-toxin. It won't affect you long term, but for our journey it will shrink you down to the size of a tall blade of grass, so you can experience the *Great Green Tree* and meet all of its inhabitants. You can only do this if you're my size. I have climbing gear, a helmet with a headlamp, and spiked shoes for you to wear. But look how small this stuff is. You certainly can't wear it right now. I need to shrink you." Webster hops down from the honeysuckle blossom, scales the branch, and marches through the grass to the foot of the first rung on the white ladder. He climbs high enough to reach eye level with Shea again.

She is standing at the base of the tree beside Webster. Her arms are folded and one hand is raised—she taps her chin while thinking. "I don't know," she says. "I do like danger, but I'm nervous about this. I hate to admit it, but I'm a little bit scared."

Webster stares long and hard at Shea. "Look, you've done wrong to so many people and animals that everyone around you is giving up on you. If you're not ready to give up on yourself then it's time to come with me." He stops talking. Peeking around Shea's shoulder, he whispers in her ear, *"You're all alone, child."*

Another easterly breeze picks up, blowing Shea's long, dark brown hair around her face. She brushes it away from her eyes for a clear view of Webster's satchel filled with miniature climbing gear.

He leans into the rung of the ladder and looks back at her. "It's time to embark on your grandest adventure yet," he says. "However, I can't *make* you do anything. You have to be strong enough to answer some tough questions about yourself concerning the bad decisions you like to make."

Shea looks down at Roland, the horned beetle, and kicks a bit of loose grass and dirt over his body. Turning back to Webster, she extends her left arm. Her thin, short fingers uncurl from a fist and she rests her open hand on one of the rungs on the ladder. "I'm ready," she says nervously.

Webster pushes his glasses up the shaft of his nose back onto his eyes. Shifting his jaw back and forth, he unlocks two miniature fangs, picks up his satchel of climbing gear, and walks across

Shea's hand. A small fuzzy pouch near his mouth opens and his fangs fall forward. Anticipating the pain, Shea clenches her other hand into a fist so tight that her knuckles turn bone white.

BITE.

Webster sinks his fangs into Shea's palm.

The pain is even greater than she anticipated. Shea scrunches her nose and squeezes her eyes closed then jerks her body, slamming her clenched fist into the ladder. She is having a violent reaction to the shrivel-toxin. Her once olive-toned skin complexion is turning a yellowish hue. She looks down at her feet and they, too, have begun changing. Her toes and feet shrink so much that her shoes fall off. Meanwhile, her arms and hands tingle while shrinking. Shea's heart is racing. She breathes deep, but can't catch her breath. The backyard spins like she's on a ride at an amusement park. Afraid she might vomit, she closes her eyes again, hoping the sensation will end soon. Just as she thinks she's going to pass out, the spinning sensation ends and she opens her eyes to find she's face to face with Webster who's balanced atop a tall blade of grass.

"You did it!" Webster says.

"I did," replies Shea, completely bewildered. The lightheaded feeling quickly passes and she regains her balance.

Webster has a wry smile. "Are you ready to take the journey I promised?" he asks.

Shea nods, still staring at her tiny fingers in amazement.

Webster turns and shuffles over to the honeysuckle bush. He pulls a pair of black-framed glasses from his satchel and scurries back, handing them to Shea. "You're going to need these. They are called *Tree See Glasses*," he informs her. "Unless you have these honey's on, you won't be able to see a darn thing inside the tree. Without them, this is just an ordinary tree."

"So that's why you wear these things?" Shea says.

"Well, yes. But I can't see well either. Mine are prescription. Yours are standard issue," Webster replies. "C'mon, put 'em on."

Shea puts the *Tree See* glasses on, followed by the climbing gear then digs her pickaxe into the first rung of the ladder in the *Great Green Tree*. Night has fallen and she can only see the first branch above her. She stares up into the dimly lit tree, but she isn't the only one. Dozens of glowing, yellow eyes are peering over tree limbs, *staring back at her*.

CHAPTER THREE
A RESPONSIBLE CLIMB

Halfway up the ladder, working up another sweat, Shea realizes that climbing is harder than it looks. Webster is having a much easier time scaling the ladder with his sticky-bottomed legs. With every plunge of the pickaxe into the wood, Shea lets out a whimper trying to catch her breath. Webster, steadfast in his climb, turns to the right where she's busy burying her pickaxe.

"I couldn't make this climb easy for you. The first step in any great journey is always the hardest," he says, smiling. "It will get easier," he assures her. "I promise."

As Shea continues her climb, she takes small breaks on each rung of the ladder. Looking back at her house, she wonders what her brother is doing right now and what he would think if he knew she was five inches tall. Back in the real world, she often made *him* feel small—now the shoe is on the other foot.

Webster takes a seat beside her, pausing to adjust his glasses again. "Do you think you're a troublemaker, Shea? I was given a large file chronicling your recent antics, but I only skimmed it. I'd rather hear it from you—straight from the horse's mouth, as they say."

Confused, Shea looks up into the tree and replies, "There are horses up there?"

Webster shakes his head and buries his face into two of his legs. "No, no horses up there. You. You're the horse giving the account of your actions."

"Are you calling me a horse?" Shea asks.

"Oh, never mind." Webster sighs. "Just answer this for me: do you think you're mean to people?"

"I can be. I suppose sometimes I am, probably—yeah," she says. "But I have good reason to be! It's because of *you* guys. You and your bug friends."

"Yes, I heard the story," he says. "Trust me, those responsible were given swift and proper punishment in the Great Green Tree." Webster nods reassuringly.

Shea closes her eyes and lowers her head. "They…they attacked me—those centipedes. I was always so nice to bugs and insects. Mom sent me for a bath, and I was getting the water ready. I don't know if the water scared them or what, but dozens—maybe even hundreds—of them came out of the drain racing toward me. I screamed. And before I could get my foot out of the tub, one of them bit me!" A tear falls from Shea's eye and drips on the rung. "It hurt! I didn't do *anything* to them. I screamed for my

Mom. She ran into the bathroom and got rid of them. But most had already scurried back down the drain, and then she yelled at me for overreacting and scaring *her*."

"I'm sorry for that. I truly am, Shea. I am here now to show you that we're not all bad. Please keep an open mind," Webster pleas.

"Yeah, well, we'll see," says Shea. Before thrusting herself back onto the main rail of the ladder, she looks up trying to catch a glimpse of the yellow eyes she had seen from the base of the tree when their climb began, but they're all gone now. Only blackness lies ahead.

"Are we close, Webster? I'm getting a little tired," she says.

Webster nods. "Oh we're close."

The faint glow of a dim light appears overhead. She throws her pickaxe over the top rung and pulls her body up. Once they reach the top, she flops down on her belly then rolls over onto her back. Her tired arms are dead weight at her sides. It takes a few moments for her to catch her breath, but once she does, she sits up slowly and looks around at the lanterns strung from branch to branch. Shea let's out a huge sigh of relief. "Whewwwwww," she says. "I thought those were eyes looking down at me! They're just lanterns."

Webster laughs. "You mean *these* eyes?"

Shea turns to find a handful of red ants lined up in a row ready to greet her.

"Welcome to the *Responsibility Enchantment Branch*!" an ant shouts. "I'm Foster, group leader for the fire ants, and servant

to Queen Felonia—queen of our nest, and mother to our children."

Shea is speechless. She can't even mutter a sound.

"Glad you could make it, Shea Stonebrook. I've been told that you don't like doing chores, and that you'd rather spend all of your time playing rather than taking care of your responsibilities. Well, look around you, my dear. We're busy, because we *have* to be. If even one ant neglects his duties, the whole colony suffers."

Many more fire ants appear while he's speaking. They're each carrying a load of twigs or bits of food. Some of the larger fire ants are carrying egg cases in their dark-red jaws. They are moving in all directions. It's like a busy highway without the double yellow lines or passing lanes. Webster leans against a branch and crosses his front legs. He's beaming and can barely control his excitement. "Quite a sight here, isn't it Shea?" remarks Foster. "Us ants scurrying every which way, carrying food and supplies for shelter—all sorts of cool things in our mouths. Do you know why we do that, Shea?"

"Because it's your job?" replies Shea.

Foster raises his arms and nods in agreement. "*Because* it's *our* job," he repeats. "Yes, you are absolutely correct. You see if we don't collect materials for our shelter, and we don't collect food or transport the eggs, our queen, Felonia, could perish. And if Queen Felonia perishes, we *all* perish. We work for one another here. We share duties, much like a human household shares duties. You and I are more alike than you think."

Webster claps in support of Foster's speech, accidentally knocking his glasses off in the process.

"Why let one person do all of the work, when you can share the work and accomplish more even faster!" Foster says. "And then no one gets too tired to carry on. Why should your mom and dad do all of the housework? They're very busy keeping food on *your* table, and a roof over *your* head. Don't you think they're exhausted at the end of the day? They need *you*. Much like Queen Felonia needs *us*."

Shea is surprised by how much sense Foster is making. "I…I never knew," she mumbles.

Webster's smile grows. He points at Foster, "You're on fire, my man. *No pun intended*."

Foster takes a seat on a workbench next to one of the ant exits. "The fire ants use these workbenches to dress and clean the egg cases that they carry from Queen Felonia's housing chamber into the incubation room. Great care is taken in transporting the eggs, and for good reason. The eggs are the lifeblood of the fire ant population in the *Great Green Tree*."

Shea removes her helmet and light, setting it on the floor next to her feet. She asks Foster if he'll move to a workbench closer to her.

He nods.

Shea asks Foster, "So how did you end up here in the tree? How did you get to be the group leader for the Responsibility Enchantment Branch?"

"Great question," quips Foster. "We didn't always live here in the *Great Green Tree*. No. We were a nomadic bunch. For the longest time we lived in the forest floor near a fast-flowing creek.

Our underground home was a mixture of sand and dirt, which we built into a small hill then carved vast tunnels and rooms deep within. The work was not easy, but as I said before, it had to be done." He scratches his chin then continues, "After a long stretch of continuous food foraging, and twig lifting, my ant soldiers grew tired. We got lazy. We assumed we had collected enough for the queen's nest and for the hill. But we couldn't have been more wrong. The weather grew fierce, and it became too extreme for even our bravest of harvesters. The supplies of the nest depleted, and our queen wasn't getting the nourishment she needed. Many of the eggs didn't make it, and our once sturdy anthill became brittle. The queen was very sad. We had failed and let her down."

From the dark corner of a thick branch, an enormous ant emerges, slowly making its way toward Shea, Webster, and Foster.

"Queen Felonia!" Foster bellows. "You should be in bed. This is your rest time. It's not the hour to—"

"I want to see the child," interrupts Felonia. "This is our first visitor in many years and it's worth my time to introduce myself."

Queen Felonia is much taller and heavier than Foster and the rest of the ants. Her wings are silky and transparent, like large sheer curtains—or two delicate, opalescent flags—spread neatly across her back. She turns her attention to Shea and addresses Foster's story. "Everything Foster has said is correct, my dear. My soldiers did let me down, and it weakened the colony. But a very magical thing happened shortly after." She glances toward Webster who is still leaning against a branch. "We met *him*," She says, smiling. "Webster was sent to us by the Governing Council.

And, knowing our peril, guided us to relocate here to the Great Green Tree where my colony of soldiers were trained on how to maintain responsibility." Felonia turns back toward Shea. "He's a very special man. He's the best guy we know," she admits. "He saved us. You just happen to be his first *human* pupil."

Webster blushes then winks four of his eyes at Felonia.

Shea is still on the workbench sitting on her hands. The shimmering glitter of the starry night sky is in full effect. A breeze picks up, rustling the leaves and swaying the yellow lanterns from side to side.

Queen Felonia looks intently at Shea. "Once the Governing Council sent for us and my colony corrected the error of their ways, Foster proved he could lead the group. They've been nothing short of amazing ever since. We have a thriving colony now, with new members being born all of the time. But let me tell you, Shea— accepting and exercising responsibility was required to achieve all of this. You have the same opportunities to contribute in your own home. If you fulfill your responsibilities, you'll see what a thriving household you can have. Your parents will certainly appreciate the effort, but it's entirely up to you, Dear. We're just here to show you how doing your part makes life better for everyone."

Webster dislodges himself from the leafy branch he's begun sinking into while trying to get a better view of Queen Felonia's living quarters. The arched entrance is lined with acorns. He scampers over to where Felonia is standing and whispers, "May we take a peek inside your most secret lair? I've always wanted to see how a queen lives."

Queen Felonia smiles. "That can most certainly be arranged. Follow me, everyone."

Webster, Shea, Foster and Queen Felonia walk briskly past the acorn-lined walls of the entrance hall. The acorns are stacked closely together, tight and sturdy—strong enough to withstand the highest winds. The hall opens up into a cavernous chamber and Felonia directs them inside one by one. Shea and Webster's jaws drop in awe of the scene. Foster stands tall with pride while everyone admires the handy work of his construction crew. Smooth, shiny acorns line everything from the floor to the ceiling. Rows upon rows of chestnut-colored shells wrap the room in striped patterns like the exposed rings of a tree.

"All of the acorns you see were graciously donated by Arthur and Bertrand, the acorn weevils," announces Felonia. "Shea, I'm sure you'll become quite familiar with them along your journey. Make no mistake; these acorns are of the highest quality. They were polished and fortified with tree bark resin from the Butternut tree. These walls keep my eggs safe and guarded from uncertain weather. I'm so very thankful for the generosity of Arthur and Bertrand."

Shea pauses from admiring the swirl pattern in the ceiling to address Queen Felonia directly, "This is incredible. I had no idea you all lived this way."

Queen Felonia takes a few steps to her right, reaches down into a woven tree-bark basket and pulls out an old egg casing. "Shea, I want you to take this casing. Keep it in your backpack as a memory of the time you spent with us here in the Enchantment

Branch of Responsibility."

Shea senses the special nature of the gift. "I will," she says. "And thank you."

Webster notices the fire ants standing guard outside Felonia's private chamber. He looks down at his watch and clicks his lips then snuffs the lanterns for the night. "Shea, we have to go," he says.

Queen Felonia escorts Webster and Shea to the door. They make their way back towards the workbenches. Felonia waves goodbye from beneath the arched entrance to her chamber then disappears within. A new ladder had appeared during their absence stretching much higher along the trunk of the tree.

Foster follows Webster and Shea to the base of the ladder. Extending a hand for a polite goodbye shake, he says, "It was a treat meeting you, Shea. I hope you take full advantage of the incredible learning opportunities within the Great Green Tree. I'll be rooting for you the whole way."

Shea gathers her hiking gear in preparation for the next climb. She grabs her pickaxe, slings her backpack over her shoulder then adjusts the light on her helmet.

Webster grabs his handkerchief and cleans the lenses on his glasses. "Up we go," he says.

Shea digs her pickaxe into the first rung of the new ladder then stops and shouts, "Goodbye, Foster—thanks for everything!" The rest of the fire ants still attending to their duties, stop and wave in unison.

Climbing side by side, Shea turns to Webster and asks, "How

come you never mentioned Felonia on our way up?"

Webster pauses then winks, "She's a queen. You *never* discuss royalty."

CHAPTER FOUR
LUNA'S MANOR

It is still nighttime in the Great Green Tree as Shea and Webster begin their ascent to the next enchantment branch. Climbs like this are easy for Webster, whereas Shea is struggling and often trails behind. Webster is pleased by the strain it puts on Shea. Pressing on despite hardship teaches discipline and the value of perseverance. Webster knows the reward is great, but he can't just hand it all to her. There's no denying that Shea Stonebrook needs some cold, hard discipline. A journey like this can't be a walk-in-the-park, easy peasy, piece of pie. After everything that Shea had put people through—no, Mam! Webster knows exactly why he was sent to guide her through the tree and her struggle is an important part of inspiring the change of outlook she needs. Shea groans again, and Webster smiles.

The night air is mild, but not warm enough to remove her

climbing gloves. Shea glances down at a faint hue of yellow light and wonders if the fire ants had left lanterns on by mistake. Webster is no help. Moving up the ladder, he keeps a spider's pace. Shea has lost all estimates on time. Now that she's entered a bizarre time warp, it's anyone's guess. All she knows for sure is that she's following a *blind* spider up some magical ladders.

"Keeping up?" asks Webster.

Shea yells, "My feet hurt! I don't have eight legs like *you*. But it's okay. At least I'm not blind!"

"That's true," Webster nods. "Yet with two *working* eyes, you still can't see what's right in front of you. Even a blind spider like me still knows what's coming."

Digging her axe into the ladder rung, Shea shakes her head at Webster and groans with disgust. "You don't know anything about me!" she barks.

"Well, I know one thing," Webster says. "I know you're a stubborn, impolite little girl who is due for a rude awakening."

Shea grunts. "Talk about *rude*," she mumbles. She's tired, cranky, and irritated to be climbing on an empty stomach without much rest. But she continues on. Every few seconds she wipes sweat beads from her forehead, shaking her hand dry with a flick of her wrist. She yells ahead to Webster, "Do we ever get to rest on this trip?"

Webster chuckles, stops climbing, and turns to look back at Shea. "Sleep? This is a tree of knowledge and hope! There's no time for sleep… But," he continues, pointing his front leg at Shea, "I can make an exception for you since you're only 10. I know a wimpy kid when I see one. And you, girl, are a wimp!"

Shea wants to hurl a nasty word or two at Webster, but she refrains, and digs her pickaxe deep into the ladder's firm wood rung. A bluish colored light bounces off a tree limb up ahead. For a moment, she's sure she glimpses the end of the ladder. Just as Shea is about to demand confirmation from Webster, he turns around and gives her what she interprets as the spider version of "a thumbs up" with his upturned leg.

Either way, they're close.

Within the time warp, night is already creeping towards daybreak. The midnight black surroundings are changing shade and crude shapes are coming into focus. The black night sky turns navy blue and hues of soft gray are breaking over the horizon. Webster and Shea stop to admire the last visible stars twinkling between the leaves and branches of the Great Green Tree.

"Beautiful, isn't it?" says Webster. "I suspect you don't usually notice what nature has to offer. You're too busy worrying about yourself to appreciate what Mother Earth has given to all of us."

Webster inhales deeply then exhales slowly. He continues looking up, gazing at the dimming stars. "No matter how many times I see the night sky, it never gets old. It's quite magical, Shea. It reminds me how tiny we all are down here—whether shrunk by shrivel-toxin or not. No matter how small the creature, we can all make a positive difference in this world, especially for those around us."

He glances toward Shea and asks, "Don't you think it's

magical?"

She shrugs. "It's alright."

Clearly, Shea doesn't see the value in Webster's perspective. Her lack of caring and propensity for narrow-mindedness really aggravates Webster. Still, he is bound and determined to make her understand the error of her ways. In more ways than one, he wants her to see the light.

Orange sunlight cuts through wisps of early morning clouds, growing brighter as Shea and Webster get closer to the top of the ladder and the second enchantment branch. Beams of light burst through the branches spotlighting their trail. Webster can hardly contain his brown, furry body from shaking with excitement. He loves daylight. It reminds him of all things joyful. The sunlight is a beacon, and to him, it stands for life, illuminating the pathway for hope.

Shea, on the other hand, is just happy she can see without a helmet light.

Webster passes the highest rung of the ladder. "The top!" he announces.

Shea's helmet is slick from sweat; it slips down in front of her eyes blocking her view of the enchantment branch. She lifts the helmet above her brow and catches a peek of the breathtaking environment. She pulls herself above the last rung in the ladder and sits down, giving her arms and legs a much-needed rest. All Shea can do, besides catch her breath, is look around the branch in awe.

"Worth it?" asks Webster.

"This is pretty cool," Shea says.

Like a slow typewriter, she moves her head from side to side gazing in awe of the botanical garden that hangs before her. Broad, lush, dark green leaves flanked by dangling vines, curl like rotini noodles. Scattered throughout the vines are bright purple flowers with black and yellow stems. The flowers weave in and out of the broad leaves, petals open wide. It is a very inviting scene. Webster and Shea feel welcome.

"What's this place called?" asks Shea.

There is a shuffling of the leaves.

"*Luna's Manor,*" whispers a voice. "I'm Luna."

Startled by the voice, Shea snaps her head around. She's face to face with the prettiest red ladybug she's ever seen.

Webster wants to say something, but he's too busy laughing at Shea's frightened reaction.

"I'm sorry to scare you, child. I didn't mean to. These leaves are thick and it's hard to know when someone arrives. Let's have a proper introduction. I'm Luna, leader of the Illunalites and caretaker of the *Good Manners* Enchantment Branch. And you, you're Shea Stonebrook—am I right?" Luna smiles.

"How'd you know?" asks Shea.

"Your presence here is well known," Luna replies. "You're the first visitor we've had in a long while. And judging from the lengthy notes we have on you, we have a lot of teaching and you have a lot of learning to do."

Webster had calmed down and taken a seat on a padded broad leaf jutting out from a wall of undergrowth. He has no intention of talking, knowing Luna has plenty to say.

Luna invites Shea to get comfortable and take a seat. Shea peels off her climbing gear and removes her helmet. In the foreground, Shea can see segments of the leaf wall opening and closing on its own. Smaller, faster ladybugs are moving about traveling in and out. Passing by Shea, they each greet her with a friendly, "Hello, how are you? Good day to you."

It's a very friendly atmosphere. This is not something that Shea is accustomed to. Certainly she is not polite like this back at home. "Why are the ladybugs being so nice to me?" Shea asks Luna.

Luna outstretches one of her short, black arms. "Well, these are my Illunalites. There are eighteen of them. They're courteous and have excellent manners. It's what we practice here. As I mentioned before, I'm their leader. I'm the head teacher and author of the *Good Manners Handbook*." Luna turns her back to Shea, pointing out her nineteen spots. "There is one spot for each ladybug here. So that makes *me* the nineteen-spotted ladybug."

Shea stands up from her padded broad leaf and points to the wall of greenery. "How are those leaves moving by themselves? Those ladybugs move in and out as they part, but no one moves them. They just… move."

Luna giggles. "Those are courtesy leaves. They only move when you're courteous to them. You can try using a knife, sword or hedge trimmers, but they will not break and they will not move for you. Can you think of a way to part them, Shea?" asks Luna.

"No," replies Shea.

"You ask politely," Luna responds. "I'll show you."

Luna, Shea and Webster walk over to the thick wall of broad leaves and vine flowers. Standing in front of a leaf, Luna tells Shea to move the leaf out of the way with her hands. Shea tries with all of her might, but can't get the leaf to budge. How could such a thin leaf not move an inch? Shea exerts all of her aggression and force, but nothing works. Luna explains to Shea that here they use good manners to accomplish everything. They don't use fancy cutting tools or hatchets to cut down the vegetation. Luna steps in front of Shea, and politely speaks to the leaf, "Please move aside so that we may enter."

The dangling vines and broad leaves slowly part like the velvet curtain on stage before a school play. Shea can't believe how easy and quickly it happens. Her jaw drops in amazement. Webster and Luna silently high-five each other behind Shea's back.

"HOW. DID. YOU. DO. THAT?" Shea asks.

Webster pipes up, "By being courteous! It's remarkable what you can accomplish if you use some good manners and are courteous to people. Don't you ever notice back home that when you're not nice, people are less likely to help you?"

"He's absolutely right," Luna says. "I teach morning classes in good manners at the Leaf of Language School. It's an etiquette class held in the education wing of this branch. Three times each week we gather to study effective techniques for communicating with other members of the Great Green Tree, *and* with each other." Luna continues, eager to tell Shea about life as a ladybug. "You see, the Illunalites are extremely social creatures. At night, we

huddle together and enjoy deep slumbers where disturbances are viewed as rude. We need uninterrupted sleep to recover from the hectic life we lead during the day. In the morning, we help polish each other's spotted shells with fallen broad leaves and drops of dew. It helps to keep us shiny and ready for flight. After our cleaning, and on days off from school, we meet in the Ladybird Café for general tree speak and updates on current events."

Shea is having trouble wrapping her mind around all of this. She had no idea that ladybug life was like this. She thought they were just boring little red insects, aimlessly wandering around. But in fact, Luna and her Illunalites are busy creatures who practice good manners and treat others with courtesy.

While standing before the now parted wall of leaves, Shea peeks inside and glimpses the beauty of what lies beyond. There are more purple flowers, every one more vivid than the next. Many branches are lined in a thin layer of green clover, creating a soft path for the Illunalites delicate feet. Off to the right, beyond an especially large purple blossom, is a rock-lined pool of water.

Webster has to clean his fogged up glasses to get a clear view inside the Good Manners Enchantment Branch. Just like Shea, this is *his* first visit too. He seems especially curious about the rock-lined pool as well.

"That's the Tub of Tiny Droplets," says Luna. "It's a very special place for us. After a long day of teaching, learning, and scurrying about, our bodies need a soak. No matter if it's sunny or cloudy, the Tub of Tiny Droplets stays full. The water comes from above, way high up in the Great Green Tree." Luna guides Shea and Webster to the tub for a closer look.

It's the clearest water Shea has ever seen. And all around the tub the air smells of fresh flowers. She can see how relaxing it must be. "This is all really nice," Shea admits. "I never realized that doors can open up when you're nice to animals or people. I never would have imagined that anyone could get past a wall of thick vines without using a cutting tool.

"Yep," Luna nods in agreement. "It's *that* simple. You'd be amazed what happens when you're courteous and use good manners. People will treat *you* differently because of it." Luna walks in front of the wall of leaves with Shea and tells her to give it a try. Shea respectfully asks if they can pass, so they can head back to the magical ladder. The twisting vines and broad leaves oblige her polite request moving aside for the trio to exit. Shea smiles and Luna gives her a wink. "See," Luna says. "*Simple*. I want you to work on that."

On the entrance side of the wall of leaves, the eighteen Illunalites stand side by side in a horizontal line. Beginning on the left, each extends a small, black hand to Shea. She isn't quite sure what they want her to do. Webster nudges Shea forward and makes a handshake gesture to help clue her in. Pursing her lips to one side, she is a bit embarrassed. "Oh," she says, and then jumps forward to greet the first lady bug in line.

One by one, Shea moves down the line, shaking the hand of each Illunalite. Every tiny handshake is followed by a unique goodbye:

"Take care."

"Safe travels."

"Thanks for coming."

"Glad you came."

These special goodbyes continue until she finishes the handshakes and proceeds to the first rung of the next magical ladder. As Shea prepares herself for another ascent, one of the Illunalites whispers to the wall of leaves causing it to part. One-by-one they all disappear onto the clover-covered branch floor within.

Webster joins Shea at the ladder and looks to Luna, "It's time for us to move on. Thanks for allowing us the unique experience of learning about your enchantment branch."

Luna bows her head and replies, "It was my pleasure." She then addresses Shea, "I'll expect you to work on your manners and start being courteous."

Hands in her pockets, staring at the ground, Shea perks up and glances toward the botanical garden. "I'm going to turn a new leaf!" she says, feeling clever.

This pleases Luna, both her and Webster laugh.

Luna waves a final farewell and Shea digs her pickaxe into the ladder. After one last cleaning of his glasses, Webster joins Shea for the next climb higher into the Great Green Tree.

With the sun shining brightly above at the highest point in the sky, Shea is slowly, but surely, beginning to see *the light*.

CHAPTER FIVE
BULLY FREE ZONE

As usual, Shea trails behind Webster as they travel up the third magical ladder heading deeper into the Great Green Tree. Webster's eight legs give him an advantage. But Shea still hasn't found a way to climb faster and often wonders why the ladder doesn't shrink to accommodate her new size. But nothing about this journey has been easy, so why should this part be any different.

Meanwhile, up ahead, Webster is noticing that the magical ladders are growing longer with each new climb. Perhaps this is a way to test and bolster young Shea's mental strength, and maybe even Webster's as well. Though Web is Shea's guide through this enchanted world, he too, is a first time climber and guest of the tree. His entire life has been spent living in the grass kingdom far below, following in the footsteps of all previous generations. He is learning new things, right along with Shea.

It is a bright, clear day. Small, puffy white clouds polka dot the blue sky, and a generous breeze flutters through the tree leaves. Shea's long, dark hair hanging below her helmet blows in every direction. In the distance, she can hear the soft, muffled echoes of chirping birds. The sounds aren't coming from all directions, though, as would normal bird chatter while they fly around the yard. These chirps are only coming from one direction... *up*.

"Are those chirps coming from the next enchantment branch?" asks Shea.

"No," Webster says. "They're a long way off. You have much to learn before you reach those heights. Remember, Shea, this trip is about the journey, not the destination."

Webster is a bit more business-like today; he isn't joking around with Shea as much as he had during their previous climbs. He knows they are still only in the first phase of his assignment, and that it's going to take a lot more determination and willpower to accomplish the goals that the Governing Council had assigned to him.

"I have a question," Webster says. "How are you feeling about the bugs and such? I mean, you met Foster, and you met Luna. They're bugs. You've even been around me for a good bit of time. What do you think of us so far? Are we *that* bad?"

Shea slams her pickaxe into the wooden ladder rung while contemplating her response. Her top lip curls a bit, "I still think you're gross," she says, smirking. "But you're a nice gross, not a gross-*gross*. I thought I'd be more afraid of you, or the others, being that we're all sort of the same size, but no one's tried to eat

51

me yet."

"Ohh, we're not going to eat you, Shea. Don't be silly." Webster chuckles. "Besides, you're too sour. We need you to be *sweet*." He winks.

Shea looks mortified. She isn't sure if he's serious or not.

Webster tilts the front of his head towards her as if he were tipping his cap. It's his attempt at being mysterious about what he knows that she doesn't.

It works.

The two stop briefly to catch their breath. Webster takes a moment to admire the view. They are only just past the second enchantment branch on their way to the third, but boy, the sights are cool. Everything on the faraway ground below looks tiny, like distant specs on stadium greens viewed from the highest seats. Leaves form tighter clusters the higher they go, offering more shade and cooler temperatures. It's still warm, though, and the thick air wraps around his body like a blanket. He is in awe of the mystical place that he'd heard so much about while growing up. Indirectly, he's indebted to Shea for the Governing Council giving him the opportunity to be her tour guide. Webster glances over and gives her a brief smile of appreciation then stares off into the clear, blue sky before preparing to leave. "Not far now," he says. "We're nearing the third enchantment branch. I must warn you, though; the creatures of this branch aren't cute. They tend to have a bad reputation down below, but their message is meaningful. I hope that you really pay attention and absorb what they have to say. They're a powerful group who didn't always live here. And to be honest, I think their message is one of the most important."

Shea appears concerned by his vague description. It's clear she has some questions. They continue moving up the ladder, but Shea is climbing at a slower pace than usual. "Who are these creatures?" she finally asks.

Webster answers briskly, "Siafu."

Even the name sounds exotic and intimidating. Shea jerks her head back as if Webster were talking about aliens from another planet.

He continues, "The Siafu are large, menacing, driver ants from the tropical regions in Asia. They're much larger than the fire ants we met down below. Their heads are massive, and each has dark red, crushing pincers mounted to their mouths."

Shea's eyes look like porcelain dinner plates ready to explode. Nerves overtake her and her chin quivers ever so slightly. "Do they *eat* people? I don't know if I'm ready for this. I mean they're probably bigger than me, right? How fair is that!? You're making it sound like I should be afraid and that they're mean for no reason."

Webster cracks a half smile. "Bullied, I think, is the term you're looking for. Sound familiar?" he asks. "Aren't you *menacing* and *intimidating* towards kids at school who you're bigger than? Don't you act *mean* for no reason at all other than to make other kids feel threatened and scared?"

Shea gazes down at her feet with an empty stare. "But I—"

"But you what," Webster snarls. "We know everything about you, Shea—don't forget that. The Governing Council knows. They're all around you. They know what you do during recess.

53

They know about the lunch lines in the cafeteria. They know you take money from Emily Greenfield, and pick fights with the much smaller Lisa Bates."

"But they—"

Shea can't complete a response. Webster continues recounting the seemingly endless times Shea had been a bully. Just when she thinks he's about to finish, he taps one of his front legs on the other, as if counting, and continues, "And Melissa Davison, why does she keep tripping on your outstretched foot every time she gets up from her desk?" He could continue, but finally stops himself, removes his glasses and wipes them clean on the rag from under his belly. "I think you get the point," he says. "Well, look up, young Shea. Do you see that pale dust blowing wildly above us? That's where we're going. That's the Siafu's Bullying Enchantment Branch." He looks her square in the eyes and says, "That's where Cypress lives."

Shea is totally freaked out. Her nerves are fried. A flop sweat breaks out on her face and her hands begin trembling. *This* is not the environment or scenario she had envisioned for this journey. This is nothing like meeting Foster or Luna. This feels different. *She* is now the one who feels threatened. She is beginning to get a taste of what it feels like to be the helpless one. And she doesn't like it.

Ahead, just how Webster had described, Shea can see the top of the magical ladder. The winds are swirling, kicking up debris—a mixture of sand and dirt. The view above them reminds Shea of some deserts she saw on the animal shows on TV. The air is cloudy because of everything the wind is kicking up. It's difficult to see past, even with the glasses they're wearing.

The two travelers hoist themselves over the top rung of the ladder. Shea tosses her pickaxe; it lands a few feet in front of them kicking up a dust cloud. She stands up and pats dirt off her pants, creating an even thicker haze. The atmosphere irritates her eyes. The branch below her feet is covered in soot. When Shea lifts her foot to take a step, her hiking boot leaves behind a noticeable imprint much like the footprints the astronauts left when they walked on the moon. But this isn't the moon. The moon is uninhabitable. The moon doesn't have Siafu. The moon doesn't have… *Cypress*. Before Shea can remove the rest of her climbing gear, a deep, thunderous voice echoes from behind a mound of dirt.

"Girl," it says. "I'm going to approach you slowly. Do not be afraid. I do not mean you any harm."

Shea can barely stand; her knees are knocking so violently that her kneecaps bang together. Even the unflappable Webster is showing signs of anxiety after hearing Cypress' booming voice.

Cypress appears.

He looks as menacing as Webster described. Shea fixates on his thick, dark red pincers. They remind her of her mother's hedge trimmers she had used on various bushes in the backyard. The only thing they're missing is an extension cord. His body is stacked in three sections, just like Foster the fire ant, only much larger. Prickly hairs protrude from his legs, and his eyes are like oval screen doors. Shea is in awe and can barely say a word.

"So this is the mighty Shea—the playground and cafeteria bully," Cypress says. "Not so intimidating when your knees are knocking, are you, girl."

"I… I—"

"Confirmation or denial doesn't matter. I know a bully when I see one. My friends, they know a lot about bullies as well." Cypress sticks two of his legs into his armored mouth and whistles. A procession of thuds like miniature elephants stomp out to greet Shea and Webster. The Siafu line up like a menacing herd, or a hardened street gang. They all look the same with long, thick, pincers, and shiny, segmented bodies with a sparse layer of course hair. It is quite a scene for Shea and Webster to absorb. All of the Siafu are looking directly at Shea.

Cypress says, "You see, we're all bullies. Well, we used to be. Reformed now," he says proudly. "I'm sure Webster gave you a brief summary of who we are and where we're from, but let me elaborate." He directs Shea and Webster to the dirt pile and says, "Grab a seat."

Shea can't sit down fast enough. She hopes her legs will stop shaking, and is doing her very best *not* to appear scared.

Cypress begins telling the story of the Siafu. "My tribe of driver ants grew up in the tropical climates of Asia. We lived and functioned as a working community, carrying food, using our enormous population to harvest anything we could find that might be useful for our colony. The problem was that other creatures got in our way. Maybe it wasn't intentional, but we were such a massive group, we viewed them as inferior. We steamrolled over

termite villages, knocked mice communities around, invaded fat-tail rat dens, and we even made our presence felt within the human world." Cypress inches himself closer to Shea, who happens to be perched on the dirt pile. He leans in and ducks his head down to her level. "You see these eyes—these eyes that look so big, and so purposeful," he says matter-of-factly. "They serve no purpose. We're blind. We use our antennae and bodily chemicals to communicate to each other. Admittedly, we used our handicap as an excuse to terrorize others. Standing here now before you, I'm not proud of that, but it's the truth."

His right pincer grazes her cheek and Shea scoots backward.

Cypress holds position and continues. "We were causing such a disturbance within the animal kingdom and the human world, the Governing Council finally stepped in and put a stop to our bullying. A representative was sent to deliver the news that the G.C. was relocating some of us. I was the leader of the village and was immediately chosen for exile. The G.C. hand-picked a dozen more Siafu from my tribe, and we ended up here, at the Great Green Tree."

Webster and Shea are completely immersed in his story. Shea has many questions, but still fears for her safety, even though Cypress had made it clear that he does not intend to harm her.

Cypress sighs then moves his pincers side to side, stretching them out before he continues with the story of his ant clan and their eventual relocation. "The representative for the Governing Council that escorted us here enrolled us in Bully Rehabilitation Counseling, also known as The B.R.C. Program. We were informed that this is a magical place full of enchantment and lessons. To partake, we were required to pledge that we would no longer engage in any more bully-like behaviors." Cypress points at Shea and says, "We were just like you. We were aggressive and we bullied lesser beings. We needed to learn that it wasn't okay to pick on creatures we thought were weaker than us, and that bullying is wrong."

Webster's lips are pursed. He nods his head in agreement.

"Even when we arrived at the Great Green Tree, we picked fights," Cypress continues. "Foster and the fire ants greeted us, and we viewed them as our enemy. We felt we were *bigger*, *stronger*, and more *powerful* than they were, so we harassed them. It wasn't long after that that the Great Green Tree community peacefully rallied against us and formed an intervention. They forced us into the rehabilitation meetings. After countless hours of training and understanding on our part, we shed our old skin as bullies and grew into do-gooders and creatures of aid. We use our strength and power to *help* this mystical place. We feel privileged to carry large supplies with our saw-teeth, and deliver goods and essential items to and from the Great Green Tree for all of its residents."

Shea sighs with relief. She can feel the transformation in Cypress' energy through his words. Sheepishly, she raises her hand as if waiting to be called on to speak, but before Cypress can react, she speaks up, "I did... *rather*, I do feel bad about my actions towards others. I knew I was being mean and deep down I didn't feel good about it. I was just trying to make myself feel better. When I bullied others *I* felt powerful." Shea takes a deep breath and asks Cypress another question. "So how did you end up staying here? They let you stay. You must have really turned yourself around. This place is so cool. I wish I was accepted in a place like this," she beams.

"We proved our worth through action by showing everyone the caring initiative we were willing to put forth," says Cypress. "It all began by changing our point of view. Despite our handicap being blind, and despite our notions of entitlement, being hated by everyone isn't an awesome way to live. Eventually, the Governing Council saw our efforts to change and approved of our new attitude. They graduated us from the Bully Rehabilitation Counseling program and appointed us as the new coaches of the anti-bullying campaign enforced here at the Great Green Tree. I'm really thankful for the opportunity that was given to my tribe and to me. I can only hope you take advantage of the opportunity given by the Governing Council and your generous tour guide, Webster, and turn *your* attitude around as well."

Webster gives Cypress an appreciative nod.

"Basically...don't be a bully," Cypress says firmly. Bullying will do nothing but bring you and everyone around you heartache, Shea. And you're the only one who can change it. The choice is yours—please make the right one," he pleads. "We know you're not acting alone, but if you can change the way *you* treat others, it might have a positive influence on other bullies as well. You've been given this gift. Use it to your advantage! Continue the amazing journey through the Great Green Tree open to new perspectives and change. Most importantly, be thinking of ways in which you can apply our lessons to your own life."

Shea nods in contemplative agreement.

Cypress extends one of his front legs to Shea as a polite goodbye.

Still sitting on the dirt hill, she's hesitant, but Webster gives her a reassuring nod that everything is going to be okay. Slow and unsteady, she tiptoes over to Cypress and extends her tiny hand.

Webster makes a clicking noise with his mouth—a signal Shea doesn't recognize.

Cypress reacts quickly, lunging at Shea, **"I'M GONNA' EAT YOU!"** he yells.

All of the color drains out of Shea's face and she almost faints. The boom of his voice knocks her to her knees where she eventually rolls onto the ground trembling with fear.

Webster bursts into uncontrollable laughter and the other Siafu ants join in.

Still shaking, Shea is confused.

Cypress leans down, "See," he says softly. "That's what happens when you bully someone."

Shea gets the message...*loud and clear*.

CHAPTER SIX
BEEING GENEROUS

Webster fogs his dirty glasses with his breath and cleans them once again, wiping off all of the leftover streaks. The small rag he uses is starting to get dirty. He wishes someone had a washing machine he could borrow. But even though this is a magical tree, he is sure it doesn't come equipped with appliances like that!

Meanwhile, Shea is standing next to the pearly white magical ladder that leads to the next enchantment branch. She is busy fixing her flashlight helmet, making sure the straps are tight. She adjusts her climbing harness and flicks some wood splinters off of her pickaxe. Her heart is finally beating within normal range. The scare Cypress gave her had caused her heart to race faster than the horses in the Kentucky Derby. Despite the cruel nature of the scare, she knew she deserved it for all of the times she'd bullied kids at school, and even her own friends and brother.

Cypress and his Siafu are gathered nearby, standing tall and stout by their dirt hills, observing Shea as she prepares for the upcoming climb. The driver ants wait patiently for Webster and Shea to make their first move up the ladder before continuing their duties on their enchantment branch. Cypress clears his throat and directs his full attention to Shea. "One last thing," he bellows. "I'm really sorry for the scare. But I needed you to fully understand what bullying feels like. Don't be that person, Shea. You're better than that." Cypress smiles. His pincers make for an awkward smile, like he just had teeth pulled at the dentist, but it's well intentioned nonetheless. With strength of confidence that surprises Shea, he says, "I believe in you."

Webster turns to Shea and adds, "I do, too."

Shea can't help but smile. She waves goodbye to the Siafu.

Webster gives a thumbs-up gesture to Cypress, and a nod indicating that Cypress had done good. Webster is also *proud* of Cypress and how far *he's* come with his own journey. Cypress responds with a reciprocal nod then the Siafu turn their backs to the ladder and enter their dirt hills.

Shea and Webster begin their ascent up the ladder towards the next destination. For a good part of the climb, they remain relatively silent. Every so often Webster makes a comment about the beauty of the tree, and Shea nods in acknowledgment. But rarely does she speak. Shea is reflecting on the lessons she had learned during her time on the Bullying Enchantment Branch, and is having a moment of clarity. Thinking about how she felt when Cypress scared her brings to mind everyone she had mistreated and bullied, and she wonders if they felt the same. Intimidating those kids really didn't make her feel good at all, and here on the tree, *her* face had told their story.

Webster notices that Shea is deep in thought. Under normal climbing circumstances, he'd be quick to spark a conversation. But this time is different. He can tell that she had received quite a reality check from Cypress, and Webster is leaving her alone to absorb it all.

The pace up the ladder is speedier than usual. Either Shea is becoming a faster climber, or she's in a rush to visit the next enchantment branch. Either way, she is much more efficient navigating the ladder rungs with her sturdy pickaxe.

Webster, still slightly ahead of Shea, looks down at her and says, "You've been quiet down there and there's good reason to be, but look around for a moment and tell me what you see." His head is held high. Webster is bursting with joy.

It's the weather.

The gorgeous weather that lifted his spirits earlier that day has continued. Sunbeams are shining through the thick leaf growth in the Great Green Tree and speckling the branches with their radiance. Living in the Grass Kingdom for so long, Webster appreciates the value of all sorts of weather conditions. But sun, in particular, he loves the most. To Webster, the sunbeams are like little rays of hope shining on the faces of everyone in his kingdom. And hope is going to be the building block for a new way of life for Shea, and possibly a job well done for Webster.

Shea doesn't respond to Webster's question—viewing it as

rhetorical. She just continues to climb. They are nearing the top of the magical ladder, and with each leaf-rustling breeze, Shea catches a faint whiff of sweetness. It is light and flowery, with hints of honey. On more than a few occasions, Webster catches Shea closing her eyes for brief moments, enjoying the windblown scents.

"She really *is* sensitive," he thinks. "Not a monster after all."

"Shea," Webster calls out.

"Yea?"

"When we get to the top, don't throw your gear off just yet. My notes tell me there's going to be an anti-stick spray waiting for us. You have to squirt that on the bottoms of your shoes so that you don't stick to the floor."

"Where are we going? A glue factory?" Shea laughs at herself.

"No," says Webster. "But you're going to wish it was just glue if you don't spray your shoes. Without the anti-stick solution you'll never be able to pick up your feet!"

"And how do *you* know?" Shea replies.

Webster smiles down at her. "I'm the guide. I *know* everything." No matter the question, Webster always has an answer, even if only fifty percent of those replies are the truth. Webster informs Shea that they are nearing the top, and judging by the increased strength of the flowery aroma, Shea doesn't need any convincing.

"You know," says Web. "This is one of my most anticipated stops in the tree. I know who's up there, and I know what they teach. If you can master it, it's a message that will carry with you for the rest of your life. It can help make the world go 'round, Shea. It's *that* important."

"Well who's up there? I want to know!" exclaims Shea. "Why so cryptic—why are you always talking in code?"

Webster smirks. "Patience, Shea, patience." Web throws his body over the top rung on the magical ladder.

Shea hoists her pickaxe once more and proceeds to follow. But before her feet touch the ground, Webster yells, "WAIT!" Shea is seconds from planting her foot on the sticky surface of the branch, but Web stops her in the nick of time. "Oh yeah, the spray—Oops!" Shea snickers.

Webster slaps his front leg to his face and shakes his head.

Shea applies the anti-stick spray to the bottoms of her shoes, making sure to coat every inch as Web had instructed. The last thing she needs to be is stuck here. Once applied, Webster gives her the approval to step onto the sticky branch floor. Shea tests her footing by lifting her left then right shoe up in the air, ensuring she doesn't stick. All good.

Shea settles in and notices a stunning array of flowers dotting the branch landscape. Masses of vibrant yellows and purples flood the walls of the Great Green Tree. *This* is where all of the sweet, enchanting scents are coming from. And the reason she had to apply anti-stick spray to her shoes: nectar. The entire floor of the branch is covered in a thick layer of nectar. It is the sweetest smell that ever graced her delicate, young nose.

All around her are nooks with fancy engravings carved into the tree trunk. There are shapes and symbols etched above each entrance. Some are intricate nature designs. Shea wonders if they are markers or nameplates of some sort, maybe used to identify each entrance. In any case, she is impressed.

Shea—eyes wide—turns to Webster, who, not surprisingly, is cleaning off his glasses. "Who designed this branch? This is the most amazing smell I've ever encountered!"

Webster is still wiping his glasses, but looks up for a brief second and points towards the creature floating behind Shea. *"She did,"* he says.

Shea turns and finds a plump, barrel-chested, black and gold bee hovering just behind her. The bee is a bit burly and covered in fuzzy hair. Its legs are encrusted with sticky yellow pollen, and bits of nectar speckle its feet.

"It's quite a pleasure to meet you," says the bee.

Before the bee can finish her introduction, Shea interrupts. "I just want to say, your floor is awesome! I want to eat it; it smells so good!"

The portly bee laughs. "Well, thank you very much," she replies. "In case you're wondering who I am, I'm Willow the carpenter bee, and you're at the Enchantment Branch of *Generosity*."

"You seem like a friendly bee," says Shea. "The last branch I visited, I thought I was going to die from fear! I nearly passed out. There were these great, big—"

Willow laughs interrupting Shea. "No, no, let's not worry about that. You're among friends here." Willow giggles. "In my enchantment branch we focus on everything positive, showing

how being generous can uplift the person beside you, and encourage them to pay it forward towards others."

Willow is feverishly flapping her delicate wings, hovering above Shea. A few of her carpenter bee friends fly out from behind one of the carved wood dwellings in the tree trunk. They are about the same length as Willow, but more narrow. And their feet are free and clear of pollen and nectar droplets. Both bees are flying to the edge of one of the tree branches where a fresh yellow bellflower had recently bloomed.

Shea looks puzzled. "Heyyy, I know them—I think?" she says. "Before all of this crazy stuff happened with Webster shrinking me, I was sitting on my back patio and saw these two black bees circling around each other. It looked like they were playing or chasing each other. Are they the same bees I saw?" she asks.

"Indeed," Answers Willow. "Would you like to hear more about me and the rest of the carpenter bees?"

Shea and Webster take a seat on one of the broken stems in an older yellowbell flower. Shea sits with her legs crisscrossed applesauce as if she were a pre-school child waiting to hear a teacher's story. Webster is trying to pay close attention as well, but can't resist tending to the floor-nectar stuck to the bottom of his legs.

Willow slows her flapping wings, gradually allowing her body to sink towards the branch floor, where a high-back wood seat awaits her. "Those two bees are Rachel and Maple," says Willow. They run pollen-scattering missions all over the Great

Green Tree and beyond." Willow looks down at her legs and back up at Shea. "We pollinate," she says. "Among other things." Willow shakes a clumpy bit of the pollen off of her leg and takes a breath. "The carpenter bees have been here on the Great Green Tree since the beginning. My family's presence on this enchanted branch dates back many many generations. We were born with the instinctual gift of generosity. In some ways, we're responsible for the continuation of life. And not to brag, but we've turned into reasonably talented architects. What can I say? We love wood, so it comes naturally for us." Willow is using her front leg to point out all the fanciful wood dwellings her and the other carpenter bees have carved out from the various tree branches. "We're givers," Willow remarks. "We pollinate the flowers. We build homes for other creatures here. By pollinating flowers, we help bring new life to the tree and the surrounding areas within the Grass Kingdom. And above all else—Willow closes her eyes briefly and opens them slowly—we're generous," she says.

Webster wants to clap, but his two front legs are stuck together with pollen and he's busy licking them apart.

Willow crooks her brow and looks back at Shea. "Rumor has it that you're the opposite of generous back home, Shea. I hear that you're not a giver at all, and that you're selfish with your toys. I heard you even took coins from a wish fountain." Willow shakes her head. "*That,*" Willow begins, "is *not* being generous. In fact, it's stealing. But we'll address that more later."

Shea's cheeks are redder than the broadside of a fire truck. She is embarrassed and can't make eye contact with Willow.

The beautiful enchantment branch that surrounds her is a constant reminder of how the bees care for one another and for others. And Shea, well, she just feels yucky inside.

Willow moves closer to Shea, whose head is still bowed. She lifts Shea's chin up with one of her front legs and locks eyes with her. "Honey, the good news is you can *change*. That's why I'm showing you all of this and sharing my story with you. It's why Webster brought us together."

Webster makes duck-lips and throws a thumbs-up sign at Shea.

Willow continues, "My ancestors, all of the carpenter bee elders that were here before me, they're gone. But they're never forgotten. They passed down all the traits of how to be a giver and a charitable creature. And now it's my time to be the matriarch of this family. I'm passing this advice on to you, Shea, so you can hopefully use that advice back at your home."

Eyes locked on her every word; Willow has Shea's full attention.

"There's a specific reason we were chosen long ago by the Governing Council to represent the Enchantment Branch of Generosity," Willow declares. She points at Maple and Rachel, who are returning from the yellow bellflower with fresh lumps of pollen on their legs. "We were born to share." Willow turns and says, "Come here, I want to show you something."

Webster and Shea follow Willow across the nectar-covered floor towards one of the carpenter bee hollows. It is oval shaped and outlined with several flowery designs, including one special drawing, etched just above the top of the entrance:

SHEAH STONEBROOK

"You see that," says Willow. "That's yours. It's your honorary house here on my enchantment branch."

Shea scrunches her nose, hesitant to mention the funny appearance of her name to Willow. With some reservation, she glances in her direction and says, "But they got my name wrong."

Willow looks back up at the etching, and with a boisterous laugh, replies, "Hey, we are *carpenter bees*, not *spelling bees*."

Shea giggles.

Willow glances towards Rachel and Maple who are transferring the pollen they had collected from the yellow bellflower into a holding tank for future delivery to another flower. "*They* etched it," whispers Willow, pointing towards the two bees. "Rachel and Maple knew of your impending visit and wanted you to feel welcome."

Shea's lip quivers ever so slightly. She bites her own tongue, not wanting to show weakness or release the tear she feels welling up in her eye. She is touched that the carpenter bees want to be so charitable and giving. These bees that she had never met in her life, had the kindness in their heart to build her an honorary home with a custom nameplate. How cool is this? She thinks. "I don't know what to say," she admits to Willow.

Webster nudges Shea's leg and whispers, "Say thank you."

"It's okay, Webster," Willow says. "I can see her appreciation. Her eyes tell the story." Willow winks at Webster then turns to

Shea. "Before I send you up the magical ladder to your next enchantment branch, I'd like for you to leave with one last piece of advice in the form of a poem. It was taught to us from our elder family members and passed down to each generation."

"And what poem is that?" asks Shea.

Willow reaches out and gently cups Shea's face with each of her two front legs, pulling her in softly.

"Be a *giver*, be a *maker*, but never, ever, be a *taker*."

It is the simplest of mottos, but especially impactful, particularly to a girl like Shea.

Shea looks Willow directly in the eye and speaks honestly, "I think…wait, I *know* I can remember that. I'm really going to try. The kindness and generosity on this branch has been so enchanting, I really don't want to leave. I know we have to go, though," Shea says, frowning.

Webster confirms the timing for Shea's disappointment by looking at his tiny watch. He taps on the glass three times with his front leg, signaling they have a magical ladder to climb.

On the horizon, daylight begins its slow descent, reassuring Webster that it's time to move on. But prior to assembling her climbing gear and strapping on her helmet, Shea reaches into her small backpack and grabs a tiny notepad and pencil. She frantically scribbles something on the paper, as if thinking too long will destroy her confidence. She dots the period, folds the note, and hands it to Willow, who, after a brief goodbye is about to fly back to the custom carved entrance of her wood hollow.

Shea and Webster hop on the first rung on the magical ladder.

Inserting two fingers in her mouth Shea whistles in Willow's direction. "Open the note!" yells Shea, and then continues to make her ascent up the magical ladder.

Willow feverishly flaps her wings, hovering above the entrance to her home; when she finally opens the note from Shea, it reads:

Thanks for Beeing Generous.
Love, Shea

CHAPTER SEVEN
THE TRUTH ABOUT LYING

Darkness begins to surround Shea and Webster within the Great Green Tree. Shea's helmet flashlight illuminates the tree trail in front of her. Webster's too. Both are pushing forward at a steady pace up the magical ladder. With the generosity enchantment branch behind them, and a newfound friend for Shea, the two travelers are anxious to reach their next destination.

Climbing at night proves to be more of a challenge for Shea, because she instinctively wants to rest her eyes and catch some shuteye. But here in the Great Green Tree time doesn't function the same as it does back home. The hour hand on Webster's watch moves much faster here. The setting and rising of the sun occurs more frequently, which causes their visual landscape to change rapidly. For what seems like hours in the Great Green Tree may in fact only be minutes here.

Shea often imagines what time it is back at home. She wonders if her family had started to miss her. Although, to them, maybe only twenty minutes has passed. The last thing Shea remembers before being lured into the Great Green Tree is her father yelling for her to come eat supper. Time slows down so drastically, as Webster had stated, that they are probably not even sitting down to dinner yet.

In some ways, this is all still very confusing for her. How many children are summoned by a grass spider wearing supernatural glasses, and then given a flashlight helmet and invited to join him in exploring a giant tree? And now she's on a full-blown adventure with *talking insects* trying to teach her how to be a better person. At times, during quiet moments of reflection, she's not sure if this is even real.

Webster turns, looking down at Shea. "It's real," he says. "And I can hear you whispering to yourself back there."

Shea looks puzzled. She knows she wasn't whispering and she can't figure out how Webster could have heard her thoughts. They stop climbing and settle on a rung of the ladder for a short break to catch their breath.

"Everything here is real," Webster insists. "That's what your glasses are for. I want you to *see* things. More importantly, the Governing Council and your family want you to *see* things. You weren't seeing anything at home. But here, you can truly *see* what's in front of you, and we're hoping it leads you down a better path for your future."

"I do like it here," admits Shea. "I thought this was just a big old dumb tree in my backyard. People would always slow down while driving by to look at it, but I didn't understand the big deal. Now that I'm here, I'm starting to appreciate how inspiring it is."

Webster takes notice that Shea's 'moments of clarity' are happening more frequently. There is hope for her yet, he thinks.

Shea is about to continue when a miniature hurricane-like wind whooshes past her. Her hair is tangled in every direction and she has to hold onto the sides of the magical ladder so as not to fall off. She doesn't know what hit her.

Shea gasps then yells, "WHAT WAS THAT!?" Wide-eyed she looks to Webster for an explanation.

Webster lifts his chin up and points with his nose.

"Look in your hand," he says.

Shea tucks her wind-blown hair behind her ear with her right hand and finds a folded note stuffed into her left hand. "I didn't even feel anything touch my hand!" she cries. She begins unfolding the note and notices the paper is shredded on the right side—torn in a zigzag pattern.

Webster is super excited and asks what the note says.

Shea opens and reads the note. Just four letters are scrawled across the paper:

TELL

She furrows her brow and looks at Webster. "It just says *tell*."

"*Tell?*" repeats Webster.

"Yes, tell. Is there an echo up here?" Shea says sarcastically.

"That's all it says. There's no name or any other words on this thing. One minute I'm sitting on this ladder rung, and the next

I'm being blown away by some crazy wind. Then there's a strange note in my hand with a single word on it."

Webster removes the wipe cloth from under his belly and cleans his glasses. "I know who did that," he says. "It's the Sphinx Moths. I just know it's them. They're the only ones who can move with that speed and create that type of wind. I'd bet my glasses on it."

Shea is intrigued by their name and wants to know more. Webster agrees to share additional information about their species, but only if Shea agrees to keep moving up the magical ladder while he talks. Though time moves differently here, they are still on a tight schedule.

"Well, they're fast," Webster begins. "We know that. From what I gather, they're messengers. You know how you get mail at home—the mail carrier comes in his little white truck and delivers your letters? Well, that's kind of like the Sphinx Moths. They're the Great Green Tree's mailmen."

Shea looks disappointed. "So that's it? They're mailmen." Shea rolls her eyes. "Awesome," she mutters sarcastically. "Well, tell me more about these... *mailmen*."

Webster points one of his hairy front legs toward the top of the magical ladder and looks down at Shea. "Why don't you ask them yourself. We're almost there now."

Ahead, in the damp, cold, night air, Shea once again sees glowing lights. They're dim, but it reminds her of the first enchantment branch where she had met Foster and the fire ants. She remembers the lanterns that were hung from long strings, illuminating their nest. Foster's lanterns were sort of yellowish in color, though—more warm. These lights are blue, like electric blue—neon almost. They're appearance is colder, like something from the polar north. Though she is uncertain about all that lies ahead, there is one certainty: the lights are spellbinding. She has a hard time averting her gaze from their glow.

The closer to the top they get, the brighter the lights grow. A few more aggressive whirlwinds buzz past her, blowing her hair wildly out of control.

"Yup, more moths," says Webster. "They must be busy tonight."

"I've never seen anything like it," Shea says. "In fact, I don't see anything at all. I just feel the wind almost knock me over. Are we close? I need to get off of this ladder. I really don't feel safe." Shea runs her hand over her hair to smooth it again. Then increases her pace to reach the last rung of the magical ladder and the next enchantment branch. In a rare role reversal, Shea moves ahead of Webster on the ladder. Even Webster is impressed by her motivation and efficiency. She sucks up deep gulps of fresh air to replace the old air that's being expelled so quickly. With a few more thrusts of the pickaxe, Shea steadies her body at the top of the magical ladder and flings her backpack over her head. It lands with a thud on the floor of the enchantment branch. Lifting herself up, she stands tall, dusts off her shirt and tilts her helmet up above her eyebrows. "*Wow,*" is all she can say.

The entire enchantment branch is glowing with the bright, arctic blue light she had seen from below. The light is coming from "bug zappers." Yes, the kind that people hang from their porches to kill flying insects during the summer time. *That kind.*

But these zappers are different. A tightly woven metal cage surrounds the beam of light in the center of the lantern. The spacing is entirely too small for any flying insect to squeeze through and be electrocuted. In fact, the light is designed in such a way that no insect could ever get hurt. To Shea and Webster, it looks completely harmless and extremely useful. Beneath the bug zappers, and directly in front of Shea, are walls of mailboxes. They are stacked side-by-side, one on top of another. Each mailbox has a nameplate mounted on the front.

Shea moves closer to the mailboxes and recognizes a few of the names. "Look, this one says Luna!" she announces. "Foster! Look, over here, this one is Cypress'. And there's Willow's mailbox! How cool is this?" she shouts.

There are so many mailboxes; she has a hard time focusing on any one in particular. Her eyes dart left then right like she's watching a ping-pong match. There are also names that she doesn't recognize. One nameplate reads *Arthur, Bertrand and Myra.* There are other unrecognizable nameplates—*so so* many of them. One particular mailbox says *Roland,* but there are two skinny tree branches across it in the shape of an X. There is also a pyramid of acorns and a pretty purple flower arrangement with yellow bellflowers spread along the top of the mailbox. It is by far the loveliest box.

Webster is standing by the magical ladder, observing the electric blue backdrop of the enchantment branch, when Shea walks over to him and says, "Hey, how come I don't see your name on the wall? I mean, I haven't looked at all of them, but I don't see a Webster."

Web shakes his head. "I told you…I don't *live* here. I'm *just* a guide," he mumbles.

"Oh yeah, that's right—sorry," Shea says. She decides not to ask any more questions concerning him and the tree. Judging from the envious look on his face while staring at the mailboxes, it's best she leave that topic alone.

Without warning, Shea is hit with another gust of powerful wind. But this time she doesn't have the ladder to brace her body against. The speed and force of the impact spins her around like an Olympic ice skater and she falls to the tree floor below. She shakes her head from side-to-side, like a dog with wet ears after a bath, and tries to focus her eyes.

A rapid-fire greeting comes from above, "Hey! Yeah! You! Up here!"

Shea's eyes finally focus on a wild creature with marbled, sienna-brown and desert-sand camouflaged wings, flying in, out, and behind one of the arctic blue light cages. Its movements are fleeting, changing direction in less than a blink.

"You! Yeah! You're Shea. I know you. You don't know me. I'm Sydney. I'm a Sphinx Moth," she says, her words as quick as her movements. "You've reached the *Lying Enchantment Branch*." Her wings flutter in a haze of rapid movement. Blurry shapes whiz past Shea's face. More Sphinx Moths are flying past her, cutting in and out of her line of sight. "We deliver the mail," Sydney says.

"Is that why you're so fas—"

"Yes. Fast. We're fast!" Sydney interrupts Shea. "We're the fastest insects on earth. One-hundred and forty-three kilometers per hour, fast."

Webster turns to Shea and winks. "Now that's fast," he says.

Shea's head is going to spin off if Sydney doesn't slow her erratic flight patterns. Shea can't keep up any more. *"CAN YOU STOP MOVING, PLEASE?"* She asks.

Sydney breaks from her flight pattern and nosedives to the tree floor, settling her tiny feet right beside Shea.

"Better," says Shea.

"As I was saying," Sydney begins again. "We're Sphinx Moths, appointed by the Governing Council long ago to be the message carriers and leaders of this enchantment branch. They realized what an asset we could be in the Grass Kingdom because we never get tired, and because of our ability to be staunch upholders of truth! Above all else, telling the truth is the one code we *must* live by. And do you know the other reason the Governing Council chose us?"

Sydney gives her head a braggadocios tilt. "*'Cause we're fast.*"

Sydney's eyes are so squinted they're barely visible. She looks directly into Shea's wide-open eyes. "Do you know why this is called the *Lying Enchantment Branch*?"

Shea shakes her head, no.

"It's because we don't tell lies here. And the reason we don't lie is because the mail we receive and deliver to other residents of the tree must be accurate. If we get the messages mixed up or lie about the content, it can have a negative impact on the lives of those receiving the communication. We deliver hand written notes as well as spoken messages. Particularly for the spoken messages, it's important for us to tell the truth and not lie. And that's why *you're* here, for lying."

"I don't lie," Shea says.

"That's a lie! You're lying right now!" shouts Sydney. "What about your brother? You got him in trouble at your grandmother's house. You told your grandmother that Christopher said bad words when really he didn't. You lied and got him in trouble! He never said those bad words." Sydney is so worked up she can't stand still any longer. She takes flight for a quick spin around the light cages trying to regain her composure. After a few fly-bys, she takes a dive towards the tree floor. Posturing her sand-colored body in front of Shea, she takes a deep breath to begin talking again.

Fearful of another scolding, Shea takes a step back.

"Shea, let me tell you a little story about the consequences of lying," Sydney begins with a softer voice. "A few magical ladders ago, you met Cypress, the Siafu ant. He and his tribe were notorious for lying, among other things, which I'm sure he discussed with you. Many years ago when the Siafu first arrived, Cypress sent messages through us to deliver to The King of the Grass Kingdom, informing him that Foster and the fire ants were not performing all their duties and were not taking care of their egg cases." Sydney shakes her head with disgust.

"When news reached The King via *our* messenger service,

Cypress and the Siafu were praised for their honesty. The King sent a message through us to deliver to Foster. If the fire ants didn't correct the situation, they were going to be banished from the Great Green Tree. When the rumor of the fire ants potential banishment made its way back to the Siafu, one of the ants couldn't hide his guilt any longer. Eventually, feeling culpable, this ant came forward and admitted that they had sent a lie to the king through our messenger service."

Webster is completely engrossed in Sydney's story. His eyes are the size of dinner plates. The level of deceit that Cypress and the Siafu used to hurt others shocks him, and in this case, the fire ants, which happen to be their own distant cousins.

Sydney continues, now speaking to Webster. "Once The King received their letter of confession, he demanded an immediate apology from Cypress to Foster. Along with a warning that if he didn't apologize it would be the Siafu banned from the tree. For a brief time thereafter, he also appointed a committee to verify the validity of all messages sent from the Siafu to anyone in the tree." Sydney turns back towards Shea. "You see, that's one of the many unfortunate consequences of lying. The lie you told about your brother's language might not get you banned from your home, but perhaps your parents won't believe what you say anymore. And that's *the truth about lying*."

Shea looks to Webster and nods in agreement with Sydney. Webster throws a leg around Shea's shoulder.

Sydney looks back at Shea and tells her she has a surprise waiting for her. The three walk closer to the wall of mailboxes where a high-flying aerial show is underway. The stars of the performance are the other Sphinx Moths. Mailbox doors are opening and closing so fast Shea can barely keep up with the varied designs on the wings whooshing by. The lavender tip of a white-lined sphinx wing tickles her nose as it passes. Letters and notes of all sizes and colors—white, pink, orange, green—are being swiftly deposited in corresponding boxes. It's like a circus performance. Shea is mesmerized.

"Look down there, Shea," Sydney instructs.

Shea searches for a moment then sees a mailbox with her name on it; big, bold letters spell:

SHEA

It shimmers in the arctic blue glow of the lights, shining for all of the Sphinx Moths to see.

"It's honorary," Sydney says. "It's not active. But I think you deserve a reward for the important lesson you were willing to learn today. And I want you to know that you're a part of our enchantment branch and wall of communication."

Shea's smile is huge. "My own mailbox!" she cheers.

"We think you're a good kid," Sydney confesses. "And *that's* no lie."

Webster chimes in, feeling forced to interrupt the celebration because he notices that a new magical ladder leading up to the next enchantment branch has appeared to the far left of the wall of mailboxes. "Sydney, I'm sorry for cutting you short, but our time here is coming to a close. It will be daylight soon, and we *really* need to head out."

"Webster, if this were a family function you were struggling to tolerate, I might have to call you out on a lie." Sydney winks.

Webster chuckles.

"But I know that's not the case here and you're not lying! It is indeed *time to go*!" Sydney stretches her wide, beige and brown marbled wings to take flight. "*Keep your eyes to the sky*!" shouts Sydney as she takes off in an erratic escape pattern, disappearing like a supersonic jet beyond the branches—off to continue her messenger duties.

Shea packs her gear and secures her flashlight helmet, adjusts her *Tree See* glasses, and polishes the tip of her pickaxe in preparation for the upcoming climb. Webster and Shea take one last look at the wall of mailboxes, pausing briefly to bask in the comforting, arctic-blue glow of the reconditioned bug-zapper lanterns.

Several steps into the climb, Shea is overcome by a powerful whoosh of air. This time she knows it's a Sphinx Moth. In her left hand she finds another piece of folded paper.

Webster pauses his climb and addresses Shea, "OPEN IT. OPEN IT. OPEN IT." Webster loves surprises.

Shea laughs. "Calm down—my goodness!" Whereas her first note had a jagged, torn edge on the right, this note has a jagged edge on the left and two words:

THE TRUTH

Shea pulls the first note out of her pocket, unwraps it and holds it next to the new note then realizes that the jagged edges fit together like puzzle pieces. The full message reads:

TELL THE TRUTH

It was the end of the folded paper mystery. And it was the end to a visit with Sydney and the Sphinx Moths that Shea won't soon forget.

CHAPTER EIGHT
EMPERORS OF THE RESPECT RESERVOIR

The crisp air that has been tugging at Shea's clothes for the last half-an-hour is slipping away with the night sky that they are leaving behind. Just above the horizon, the dim radiance of daylight is peeking around corners of clouds dotting the skyline. Varied shades of pink and purple mix together like oil paint on an artist's palette. The sky is especially magical during dawn and twilight transitions. Colors dance in a way that even holds the attention of a 10-year-old. Dawn is a welcome site, as always, for Shea. Something about the blue sky brings out the enthusiasm in her. It is a stark contrast to the darkness, which fetches saddening thoughts of her home environment and the turmoil of the life she's been leading.

However, little by little, after each tiny victory on each

enchantment branch, Webster is noticing subtle changes in Shea's attitude as their journey progresses. He is taking mental note of how she greets, responds to, and concludes visits with the branch guides. He's even collected mental pictures of Shea smiling, and showing genuine emotion that doesn't involve frowning, scowling or pouting. It is refreshing to see. And though it is hard for her to admit that there have been changes in her attitude since the beginning stages of her journey through the Great Green Tree, she *is* flirting with the idea of a new perspective. And *this* makes Webster happy.

While climbing to the next enchantment branch, Webster looks in Shea's direction, smirks then says, "You seem *different* today."

"Different how?" she asks. "You're always analyzing me. Is it possible we can just climb and *not* talk for five seconds? My Mom analyzes me. You're starting to remind me of her."

Webster laughs. "Listen, I just meant lately you're *nicer,* not so abrasive. Honestly, I think it's refreshing. Plus, it's good timing because you're going to want to be on your best behavior for our next destination. We're almost there." Webster raises both eyebrows and stares directly at Shea. *"These guys don't mess around,"* he says.

The longer they climb, the brighter the sky becomes. The once pink and purple flashes of light that played hide-and-seek behind bands of creamy clouds have transformed into a singular light blue backdrop for their journey. Not a cloud in sight—only blue, as far as a blind Spider can see. The sun is lifting, and the temperatures are rising.

The landscape within the Great Green Tree is showing signs of change as well. With each ladder rung they pass, fewer lush, green leaves are attached to the branches. It's as if they are heading not into a tree at all, but rather, a wasteland of hibernating foliage. Webster and Shea are climbing a bit more cautiously, assessing the bleak terrain for unexpected obstacles. He knows they're approaching the top of the magical ladder and will be entering a place he has only imagined, but never viewed with his own eyes.

The two perch themselves on a ladder rung, assuming it's their last chance to rest before the final push over the top rung. Shea is nervous and turns to Webster. She has questions that have been simmering for the last half of this climb.

Webster watches the sweat beads swell, forming into larger droplets on her forehead then slide down her skin as if trying to escape something scary.

"These guys—these branch guides—what do you know about them?" Shea asks. "I didn't sign up for this tree adventure to get my head ripped off...or worse. You've made me think they're a gang of ruthless killers."

"Well...they are. Mmm, well, they *were*." Webster feels sheepish. "I didn't want to burden you with the details, but hey, you asked. The story passed down through my family of web-weavers is that these guys are Emperor Scorpions. Specifically, they're a band of brothers who grew up in the savannah of West Africa. Their leader is the oldest brother, Enzo." Webster pauses to make sure Shea is still breathing. "Originally," he continues, "Enzo and the Emperor Scorpions were enforcers of respect out on the savannah. They were a menacing group with jet-black protective plates that blanketed their bodies like suits of armor. They were tanks with legs. And the one thing the Emp's were known for was commanding respect." He leans in towards Shea and whispers in her ear, "You have to remember...these guys come from millions of years of evolution. They look and act this way because *they were born to.*"

Shea shuffles. Glancing down the ladder, she wonders how difficult it would be to find her way back home on her own. Maybe she could stuff herself into an envelope and have one of the Sphinx Moths deliver her safely into her warm bed.

Webster pretends not to notice her discomfort and continues. "Their natural desire to be in command is where the trouble started for them. Back in West Africa on their native soil, humans invaded their habitat and waged war on the Emp's, destroying their homes, stomping out all who tried to protect their lands. And from what I'm told, one moonless night, Enzo and the remaining Emp's set out on a quest to retaliate against the humans who had assaulted their brothers."

"What happened?" Shea asks.

"They crept in on a sleeping man, and with one unified motion, stung him dozens of times until multiple doses of trace amounts of venom eventually overpowered him and he stopped breathing. Enzo felt that justice had been served for the death and destruction the humans had inflicted on his brothers and their homes. And that was that...or so they thought. Little did they know, the humans were planning an even more vicious assault and the war would wage on."

Shea sits in silence.

"That's when the Governing Council stepped in to put an end to the madness overtaking the savannah. Enzo and his brothers needed to be relocated, not only for their own protection, but also for the protection of the humans. A final line had been crossed, and the Council thought it wise to move the Emp's into the Great Green Tree, where they could eventually learn effective methods for giving and getting respect." Webster removes the glasses from his face, takes out his handkerchief and wipes the lenses with the one remaining clean corner. "I'm sorry to have shared that story *right before* you're about to meet the Emperor Scorpions," he says. "But you *did* ask, and maybe it's necessary to warn you so that you're fully aware to be on your most proper behavior!"

Shea's arms are crossed and she's rubbing her left cheek in deep contemplation of everything she'd just heard. Looking around, she can see that most, if not all, of the leafy foliage is gone. She senses that very soon they are going to enter a realm that is arid and empty, void of all things *tree*. Big, tough, Shea, is now just a scared, little girl. She misses the warm, inviting environment of some of the previous enchantment branches. Like Luna's Manor, which had bloomed with vibrant flowers and plants—the same kind that Willow the Carpenter Bee had shown her. Those branches were delicately quilted from a fabric of love and understanding. This enchantment branch is stitched together with scorn and resentment.

Before she can lose herself in the dreadful visions and unpleasantness, Webster gently taps her on the shoulder and points to the tip of the ladder. With hesitation, he says, "We're here."

"I wish we had a periscope," says Shea.

"Yeah, well, this isn't the ocean," replies Webster.

With caution, Shea and Webster peek over the top of the ladder rung, just enough to view the tree floor without their heads being fully exposed. It is enough of a view to scout the terrain and observe what waits. The scene is like something out of a military movie. In two perfect, parallel lines, stand two ranks of midnight-black Emperor Scorpions armed to the teeth in shiny, onyx-colored body suits with barbed tails and black, glassy eyes.

Webster looks at Shea and whispers in her ear, "My family was right. They *do* look like tanks."

The tree floor is barren and rocky. The walls enclosing the branch are jagged and dirt filled. There are branches, but no leaves. The living quarters are dusty and arid—just like Webster's family members had described the West African savannah. This whole branch environment seems to mimic where the Emp's had once lived.

Shea turns to Webster, who is busy gulping down the lump in his throat and tries to spit out a question, "Is that—"

"NAME'S ENZO," bellows a cavernous voice that interrupts Shea. "I can't see you, but I can hear you. I *feel* the vibrations in your voice. Climb over the ladder and come forward. We Emp's have poor eyesight, and I need a closer look at who I'm speaking to."

THE GREAT GREEN TREE AND THE MAGICAL LADDERS

Without hesitation, fearful of reprimand, both Shea and Webster crawl over the top of the magical ladder and make their way towards the rows of Emperor Scorpions. All Shea can focus on are Enzo's massive clawed pincers where everyone else would have hands. He addresses the frightened travelers. "These hands— you're looking at my hands. Do you know what these hands have done?" He turns his ragged head around and points one of his claws toward the end of his shiny body. "And that tail—very barbed and very powerful. Do you know what that tail has done, little girl?" asks Enzo. "That tail is responsible for bad things. *All* of our tails have done bad things. And do you know why, little girl?"

"No, sir, I do not," answers Shea.

"Sir...*see*...I like that," Enzo says, turning to Webster. "A sign of respect." Enzo turns back to Shea and says, "I'm starting to like you already, and that's hard for me to say, seeing as you're a human. Your people inflicted so much harm on my people before we came here to the Great Green Tree. And, in turn, we caused them harm. It was a *"poisonous"* relationship," Enzo snickers. He stretches both clawed-arms out from his sides into the air as if addressing the entire tree. "But here...here we are reformed. We are...*re-born*, thanks to the Governing Council. And thanks to them, we're here...for you."

Enzo turns around to speak to his platoon of armored brothers and mutters, "At ease boys. Carry on." The bands of brothers break formation and scatter in various directions on the enchantment branch. All that remain are Enzo, Shea, and Webster.

"If you haven't figured it out yet, Shea," says Enzo. "This is the *Respect Enchantment Branch.* And just in case you're clueless, I am their leader. Based on the vibrations we heard from you and Webster on the magical ladder, I'm going to assume that Webster has briefed you on where we came from and why."

It's as if Enzo's poor eyesight has resulted in all of his other senses becoming that much more powerful. Webster looks down at his hairy legs and thinks to himself, this guy's a psychic.

Enzo returns his full attention to Shea and asks her to take a seat on the round boulder next to the dirt wall. "I know about you," he says. "Your mother, your teacher—I know about them, too. You seem to have a real problem giving your elders and family members respect."

Shea stares in disbelief that this interaction could ever end well.

He nods and says, "It's fine, answers are not mandatory...*I know*. Maybe you weren't aware of it before you agreed to step foot in this tree, but respect is something that is earned. It is *not* given."

Enzo has perfect posture, making his body appear even taller. It also helps that his body has a stretching mechanism that enables him to appear larger than he really is. Out in the wild, it serves an important purpose for intimidation of enemies and self-defense. By Shea's standards, he is towering over her. "Why did you call me sir when I first greeted you?" asked Enzo.

Shea replies, "Because you're *huge* and *scary*!"

Enzo can't help laughing and responds with a playful sarcasm. "Huge and scary, huh? Well, that's what the Governing Council was looking for to fill this position in the Great Green Tree. They thought someone like me could get the point across to someone like you if I were huge and scary. They figured a creature of my size could command respect and teach it well. Is it working?"

"Yes," admits Shea.

"Excellent!" shouts Enzo. "But the truth is, huge and scary doesn't equate to deserving respect. And you should certainly never use your size to intimidate or try to *force* respect. That's not how any of this works."

Webster purses his lips and jabs a leg towards Enzo, as if to signify they're in agreement with a high-five and mutual "yeah man!" or "right on!"

Enzo continues his lesson.

"Back when we moved here from West Africa, it took us a long time to realize and recapture the essence of giving and getting respect. We were so disappointed by the treatment we received from humans in the savannah that it destroyed our ability to even want to respect others. Honestly, we didn't care. We thought we were indestructible and nothing could hurt us. Sure, it's true, the humans trampled on our livelihood and stomped out our way of living, but we weren't exactly the most respectful creatures either. In the end, it caused nothing but heartache for us and the humans."

Enzo gently rests his pincer atop Shea's shoulder and directs her toward another area of the *Respect Enchantment Branch*. "I'd like to show you something," he says.

Shea rounds the boulder. Accompanied by Enzo and Webster, they travel down a long, dirt-packed corridor. It is just large enough for Enzo to fit through. Both sides of the corridor are built from cross sections of stone and rock. There are wooden torches along the walls spaced every six or seven feet apart to light the way. Though they are quite dim and most of the light is coming from the tunnel entrance at the end of the trail.

Both Shea and Webster have *no idea* where they're being led.

Enzo escorts the travelers into a hollowed out room complete with a stone-encrusted pool smack dab in the middle filled with crystal-clear water. Surrounding the pool are two, black-padded benches each in the shape of a half moon. "Behold," says Enzo. "My Chamber of Solitude." Enzo points to the pool. "This is the Respect Reservoir. This is *the* most important dwelling on our enchantment branch. It was put here by the Governing Council as an instructional tool to guide others in learning the importance of respect."

Shea and Webster lean over the side of the pool for a full view of the sparkling water. The surface is mirror smooth and Shea can see every freckle on her cheeks, every hair in her eyebrows, and even the chickenpox scar on her chin. It is a mystical body of water. Webster is transfixed as well. They each continue exploring their own reflection while Enzo explains its purpose.

"The Respect Reservoir is a solitary pool of reflection. It's not made to drink from. It's a device used to measure oneself against *himself,* per se. One thing we were taught, and the message I'm sharing with you today is, *in order to respect others, you have to respect yourself.* A good place to begin is taking a long, hard look at you, and then ultimately deciding what needs to change in order to respect yourself."

Enzo joins the others and sits down on the circular bench then looks down at *his* reflection in the Respect Reservoir. "When I first arrived at the Chamber of Solitude, I didn't like what I saw in the pool. I didn't have respect for myself, so how could I respect others? It was no wonder the humans and my Emperor brothers waged such a war against each other back on the savannah. No one had respect for one another. So when I arrived here, I spent time looking at myself every day in the Respect Reservoir. I thought about everything I'd lost and everything I hoped to gain and eventually, through action, my confidence to accomplish those goals grew until one day I had learned to respect myself. Eventually, I encouraged all of my brothers to spend time in the Chamber of Solitude as well, especially when they felt the urge to act out with rage or disrespect."

Enzo turns towards Shea, who is still looking down at herself in the mirrored water. "What I'm trying to tell you is, you'll ultimately find yourself alone if you continue down the path you're on—disrespecting others—particularly your Mother and your family. But it all starts with *you.* The good news is you don't need a mystical pool of water and a bench to learn how to respect yourself. *All you need is a mirror.*"

Webster stops staring at his own reflection for a moment to glance over at Shea's. He gives her a broad smile then says, "This stuff is simple, Shea. You're not moving mountains here. Every time you respect yourself or someone else, it's a drop in a bucket. You don't have to fill the whole bucket in a day. Just start with a drop here and there and eventually the bucket will overflow."

Enzo throws his right pincer in the air. "Great point!" he bellows, causing the water to ripple ever so slightly, breaking Shea's trance.

She looks up and watches Enzo as he continues speaking.

"Your Mother and your Father are hard-working people. What I gather from our reconnaissance missions is they do a lot for your family to keep the roof over your head and food on your table. They're just looking for a little respect, Shea. It's a shame that you had to go through all of this to potentially learn how to give it, but I know it's within you."

Webster nods in agreement, gently nudging Shea to reinforce Enzo's point.

"And school," Enzo continues. "Your teachers are kind of a big deal, as well, Shea. They are there to guide you—to mold you into a more thoughtful person. They're allies, not enemies. You'd be amazed at how much respect you'd get if you just showed it to *them* first. But there's a thing called tough love, too. And under no circumstance are your parents, family members and teachers going to coddle you and respect you if you don't step up and make good on giving them your respect first."

Shea's eyes well up. A single tear, just heavy enough to slide past her eyelashes, rolls down her cheek and falls into the Respect Reservoir. The single drop sends a wave of ripples bouncing off the sidewalls of the reflection pool, distorting her appearance.

Enzo winks his black-glassy eye at Shea. "See," he says. "You changed the way you look already. And all it took was a little drop in the bucket."

Shea removes her *Tree See* glasses and wipes her eyes.

"I want you to remember what I said about the mirror," insists Enzo. "Respect is *earned*, not given. Respect yourself, Shea. Start there." Enzo puts his mammoth pincers on Webster's shoulders and gives him a little shake, nearly knocking him over. He looks at Shea and says firmly, "And listen to *this* guy. He's the best tour guide I've ever met. And he seems like a heck-of-a friend to have on your side."

Enzo, Shea, and Webster leave the Chamber of Solitude and begin their trek back down the dimly lit corridor towards the main entrance hall. Upon arrival, Enzo's band of brothers are back in their two-line parallel formation, awaiting the chance to bid farewell to their guests. Beside the rounded boulder where Shea had sat earlier, another magical ladder has appeared, stretching even higher into the Great Green Tree. Shea looks up the ladder into the vastness of the tree and sees something that's been missing from this enchantment branch. *"Hey,"* yells Shea. "I see green leaves!"

Enzo nods and says, "Green…means a *new* beginning."

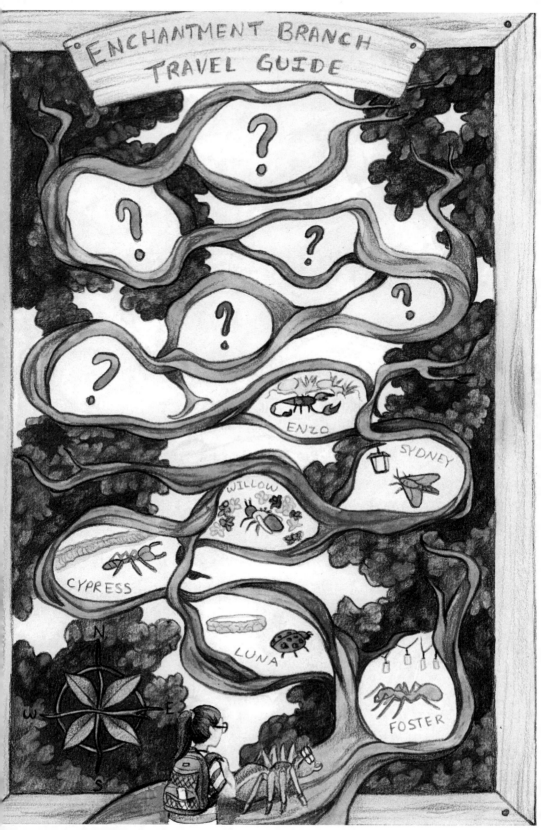

CHAPTER NINE
MORALS OF THE MANTIS

The magical ladder that Shea and Webster are scaling is one of the tallest ladders they've seen so far. It is long and skinny, and disappears far into the depths of the tree above them. And true to Shea's word, there are more green leaves, growing thicker and more vibrant with each thrust of the pickaxe and step up the ladder. The variation includes a vast array of soft greens, light greens, olive greens and pea greens mixed and intertwining—each emphasizing the next. There are patches of forest, sea, ivy and fern greens—greens that she's never seen, can't pronounce, and maybe haven't even been discovered yet.

The day is deep blue, like calm waves in the middle of an ocean. The sun's strong rays illuminate their path even through the densest areas of the Great Green Tree. The leaves glow, their veins pulsing from the magnificence of their contrasting colors.

A tender breeze sweeps through the tree causing clusters of leaves to separate, opening viewing portals to the enormous blue sky beyond. It is a perfect spring day.

Webster, as usual, is just ahead of Shea, using the advantages evolution has given him, which includes sticky, padded feet. Shea, on the other hand, is using her conventional climbing tools and sweating like a long-distance runner jogging through the desert. But none of it seems to matter. Her adrenaline is still pumping from her visit with Enzo, and she's feeling more energized than ever.

Shea throws a small pebble at one of Webster's rear legs to get his attention.

He turns around.

"I know you're just a tour guide and all, and I'm your first student—but how much does it really bother you that you can't live here? You told me when we first met in my backyard that you're not allowed to live here—that you belong in the Grass Kingdom, like all your other family members that came before you. Does that bother you?"

This is the first serious question Shea has ever asked Webster that has nothing to do with herself. The gesture and question catches Webster off-guard. He scoots over to a rung on the ladder to rest his legs and think for a moment. Shea follows and takes a seat next to him, awaiting his response.

"Well," Webster begins slowly. "When you've been around as long as I have, and as long as my family have been tree guides, you can't help but imagine living in such a miraculous place.

Despite what *you* might think of the Great Green Tree so far, it *is* a place of endless magic and wonder."

"So you're lonely in the Grass Kingdom?" asks Shea.

"Lonely? No. Maybe a bit envious of the creatures who live up here." Webster sighs. "I have quiet moments at home where I entertain the notion of having my own enchantment branch. I mean, who wouldn't? Well, *you* wouldn't. You're human. You wouldn't understand. But in here, you're a part of something truly special. Of course I'd want that. But I know my place in this Kingdom, and I'm okay with that. I just hope to do a good job with you, making my ancestors proud, and to please the Governing Council."

"Well, I don't know about your family, but *I think* you're doing a good job," says Shea. "You've treated me very fairly."

Webster is shocked to be receiving a compliment from Shea. *Has she really turned a corner?* "I appreciate that, Shea. But we really need to press on. I'm excited to inform you that we've reached the halfway point in our trip. But we still have many climbs to go."

The two re-adjust their gear, and dust themselves off. Shea shakes out her hair, and pulls her brown locks into a tight ponytail— the kind Mom taught her when she was little. Webster, on the other hand, shakes his back legs like a dog that just jumped out of a bath. No ponytail for him. They begin climbing again, but at a much smoother, and quicker pace. Webster, fleet-of-foot, hustles ahead of Shea. He is the guide, and the guide is supposed to scout out the upcoming area, which he is determined to do masterfully.

Shea momentarily stops climbing, cracks a sly smile and

yells up to Webster, who is still within earshot, "You know you're gonna get your own branch one day!"

Webster pretends like he doesn't hear her, and continues on.

The closer they get to the top of the long, skinny ladder, the lighter and brighter the immediate area becomes. The leaf clusters are no longer as dense. It's as if they are emerging from a cocoon within the tree.

"I can see the light at the end of the tunnel," Shea hollers. "What's up there, Webster? Can you see what I see? I'm seeing so many different types of light shining through the leaves."

Webster is so far ahead of Shea that he has already reached the top. He can't wait for Shea to see what he is seeing. "Hurry," he yells. "It's glass. Everywhere. Oh, you should see these colors," he shrieks.

Shea has no clue what he's talking about. She scurries up the ladder as fast as her arms and legs will take her until she reaches the top of the ladder. Once there, the beauty stuns her.

Huge stained glass arched windows fill the walls of a structure built from stark-white birch bark. Wide beams of sunlight shine through the glass casting a harmonious array of colors on the enchantment branch floor. Reminiscent of a church, each window depicts the image of a cloaked figure—heads bowed and hands clasped together.

Shea blurts the first word that comes to mind, "Praying…" But before she can continue, she's startled by a noise behind her.

"Mantis," says a robed creature standing in the hallway near the entrance. It's a male's voice, and he glides across the wooden

floor in the direction of Webster and Shea. He is wearing the same tree-trunk brown cloak as the stained glass figures with a lighter brown rope tied around his waist. As a show of courtesy, he removes his hood to reveal his Mantis head.

"Welcome to our enchantment branch, Shea. We've been expecting you. My name is Preston. I'm a high-ranking member of the Praying Mantis clergy. You've reached a very spiritual section of the Great Green Tree. Here, we specialize in moral guidance and the path of the good. *We're* the ones who encourage positive thoughts inside your little head and offer righteous assistance during times of uncertainty."

Shea is baffled and doesn't know what to say... or *not* say.

Preston slowly spins his body around and stares at a framed photograph of a rhinoceros beetle hanging on the far wall.

"Obviously, we didn't reach you in time," says a gloomy Preston.

Shea immediately knows whom he's referring to. She stares down at the floor. Ashamed, she avoids making eye contact with Preston.

Preston continues, "Here at our enchantment branch, we focus on moral accountability, and more importantly, the *ability* to avoid unnecessary killing, which you are all too familiar with, Shea. Here, that sort of disregard for the value of life is outlawed. I'm talking about the tree as a whole, not just here on this particular enchantment branch." Preston's arms are hidden inside his robe, but he raises a billowy sleeve beckoning Shea and Webster to follow. His movements are slow and steady as he travels around the room, staying close to the birch-bark wall. He continues speaking as he glides. "It's my duty to impress upon everyone who enters these hallowed halls the negative impact of unnecessary killing. Among our devout members of the Great Green Tree community, my purpose is to ensure that life is considered precious and always treated with love, care, and graced with empathy."

Preston turns to Shea with grace in his voice. "In your world, people tend to respond with aggression and without regard for consequence or feelings. You also tend to respond to a situation with no regard for consequence. As a whole, you're followers, not leaders." He pauses to take a deep breath.

"In your backyard the day that young Roland was laid to rest by the soles of your feet, did you ever stop to think before your foot came down what consequences might occur—what lives you were affecting?"

Shea looks back at the photo of Roland and shakes her head, no.

"My dear, life is a precious gift. We're all given *one*. Incidents occur within the animal and human kingdom that are not controlled by us. We die. Sadly it's a part of life. But when death occurs at the hands of another in a direct and wicked manner, that, my dear, is what we call unnecessary. And that is what *we* must stop."

Shea's voice trembles a bit, and her words are hesitant. "I...I didn't know." Her voice cracks.

"And that's why you're here," replies Preston.

Three mantis clergy members emerge from a hovel nearest a wide tree branch just past a windowless hallway. They, too, are cloaked in brown robes with hands clasped, hidden inside oversized sleeves. Making their way past Shea, they lift their heads only briefly—a somber acknowledgment—then swiftly avert their gaze back downward. It is a reverent showing of the fact that they are in a mourning period for Roland.

"Follow me," says Preston. He guides Webster and Shea out beyond the Grief Grounds, pointing out historical reference markers along the way. "This place was formed by the creators who located us here many moons ago. It's the Mercy Branch. This branch has exceptional power—the power to forgive and *be* forgiven. Because we believe creatures and humans make mistakes, it is here where you can atone for your wrongdoing."

Preston, Shea and Webster arrive at the Mercy Branch, and immediately Preston's guests are in awe of the site. The branch extends further out from the tree than any other, and is wider as well. Fig leaves and olive branches border it, and the air smells like honeydew. The floor is made from perfectly rounded acorn shells woven together by millions of silkworm strands. The shine from the floor is almost blinding, but Shea and Webster can't turn away.

Just ahead is a domed citadel type structure towering over the right side of the Mercy Branch. "*This* is Beetle Hollow," says Preston. "Beetle Hollow is our purgatory, otherwise known as the *waiting place* for violators of important laws of the Great Green Tree and The Grass Kingdom, particularly unnecessary killing." The entrance door is solid oak with long branches as handles. Above the doorframe hangs an engraved sign:

ye who enter, be not judged, be forgiven.

Preston opens the doors to Beetle Hollow and beckons Shea and Webster to enter. The cavernous dome is dotted with fat, waxy candles blanketing the room with a burnt-orange glow. Directly in front of them, leaned against the wall, sits three high-backed chairs adorned with olive branches and fig leaves. Preston closes the door and begins explaining the scene. "Those are the exalted high chairs. No—not for babies, like in your human world, but high chairs for the mantis elders who supervise the lawbreakers that reside within the Great Green Tree." In front of the chairs are three elongated candles. "Those candles are lit when a lawbreaker must come forth and sits on the wooden bench in front of the elders. Should the elders decide the accused did not fully atone for their wrongdoing, then the candles would be extinguished and the lawbreaker would face temporary banishment from the Great Green Tree. However, the most serious and harshly punished crime would be the unnecessary killing of another. And to be quite honest, we have not had that happen here for a very long time." Preston's intense gaze makes Shea uncomfortable.

"I thought this place was free from crime," says a surprised Shea.

Preston continues speaking intently to Shea. "You remember Cypress—the Siafu, and Foster—the Fire Ant, right? Of course you do. I'm sure Cypress told you about his malicious behavior towards Foster and the Fire Ants when they first arrived here. He was sent here to spend time at Beetle Hollow for bullying and harassing the fire ants. The mantis elders charged him with great dishonor, but ultimately he won their favor and was given an olive branch, only to return to *his* enchantment branch and teach others not to bully."

Shea is amazed by the detailed code of honor that the Praying Mantises abide by within this enchantment branch. She has also been made nervous by the notion that Preston's next course of action may be to put her on trial before the mantis elders.

"Beetle Hollow is not just a gathering place for those who commit wrongdoings against the Great Green Tree's code of ethics," Preston assures her. "And it's certainly not a final farewell for those who commit unnecessary acts of killing (considered to be the worst of the worst). No. Beetle Hollow is much more than that. It is, above all, a place of atonement, a place of reconcile to make up for your unlawful activity, and ultimate crime of unnecessary killing."

As they turn to exit Beetle Hollow, the cloaked threesome she'd seen earlier glide over the flats of the Mercy Branch and through the oak doors of Beetle Hollow breezing past the trio.

Preston, once again, addresses Shea, but in a slightly softer tone, "I hope you don't get the impression that I'm picking on you, Shea." "But what you did in your backyard the day of Webster's arrival was unthinkable to us. The gentle creature you took away from this tree—he was a family member—a friend—a creature of life that you irresponsibly disposed of."

On the verge of tears, Shea's eyes gloss over. She is beginning to feel sadness and remorse.

"We get it. We *know* you didn't realize he had such a precious, purposeful life with deep meaning, filled with love and people who care for him. You thought he was just another beetle that got in *your* way." Preston's tone is stern. He removes one of his hands from his elongated robe sleeves and points up into the Great Green Tree.

"But there are creatures, Shea, who mourn for him as we do. He is a cousin of the Acorn Weevils and they are good citizens, Shea. Roland was a *good* citizen. And he's gone now. We'll move on. We always do. But you needed to know that. And you needed to hear it."

Without Shea saying a word, Preston knows that his words have touched her heart. The salty tears dripping from her wind-kissed cheeks are also a good indication. Even poor Webster has trouble keeping his eight eyes dry.

Shea remains near the edge of the Mercy Branch wiping tears from her face. All she can think of is regret as she peers with remorse through the fig leaves at the vast, blue sky.

"Preston," Shea says. "Would you mind it terribly if we walk back through the entrance hall where the stained glass windows are? It's so pretty there." She knows that they will pass the framed picture of Roland. Preston nods, granting her request. The three of them slowly make their way back across the Mercy Branch until Beetle Hollow is gone from their sight.

Shea slowly approaches the picture of Roland, hanging so peacefully on the birch bark. Placing her hands and head on the wall next to the picture, she mutters something quietly that neither

Webster nor Preston can decipher. She is saying her peace in the only manner in which she knows how. It is the best she can do.

Moments later, a swift *whoosh* of air zips past her, causing all of the leaves to shake furiously. She has no idea what just happened, but she feels as if she's experienced an event like that before. It reminds her of the Sphinx Moths whizzing in and out of enchantment branches. Shea lets go of the wall, gathers herself and shuffles back across the room to join Preston and Webster by the new magical ladder that has appeared in the corner near the largest stained-glass window most prominent upon first arrival. The entire ladder is coated in shiny acorns.

Preston turns to Shea and whispers, "I have a feeling the Weevils did that. They must have somehow heard what you said by the wall. You know, around here, we mantises like to call that *an olive branch*."

If that *is* the case, Webster has a theory on how that message was received by Roland's acorn weevil family. But now is not the time. He merely winks at Shea, and prepares himself for the ladder climb.

Preston has one last piece of advice for Shea before she gears up for the new climb. Realizing she's only ten years old, he hesitates telling her the phrase he was taught when he first occupied this enchantment branch. But says it anyway.

"If death becomes shallow, then life was a gift that never was hallow."

Shea looks confused. "I don't know what that means," she says.

Preston laughs. "I figured as much. It means if you view death without a care, then life was never honored as holy. It wasn't purposeful. I want you to value all of the life around you. Give it meaning. Don't kill unnecessarily!"

Shea looks at Preston and extends her sweaty palm. "I owe it to Roland," she says. "I promise not to do that anymore—no matter where I am."

Webster cleans his glasses with his handkerchief, which, by now, is filthy and almost defeats the purpose. Webster shakes Preston's hand and he and Shea make the short walk over to the acorn-encrusted magical ladder. They are off on the next segment of their journey.

Preston raises his hand from beneath his oversized robe sleeve, signaling farewell, and Shea and Webster begin the strenuous climb to the next enchantment branch.

CHAPTER TEN

I'M NOT AT LIBERTY TO BE JEALOUS

Wind lifts and separates the leaves, revealing the dusky night sky beyond. Webster and Shea's shadows are disappearing with the sun. In this world, day and night play a game of "tag-you're-it"– one after the other taking its turn in near perfect hourly intervals. Shea has no true concept of time here. She's not sure that Webster does either, but he seems to, which makes his role on the journey that much more important. He's doing a very good job keeping them focused on the mission at hand, and getting Shea to each subsequent enchantment branch. She just wishes she could spend more time resting on each branch and meeting its creatures.

They are more than halfway through their ascension of the tree, and exhaustion is wearing on both of them, mentally and physically. Webster had suspected that the climb might become more difficult as they went, but he's surprised by how *much* harder. Both are moving up the acorn-adorned ladder at a snail's pace. If Webster had a tail, it'd be dragging. For the first time during this adventure, Webster's sticky padded feet are beginning to tighten and get sore. *This* is work.

With each new ladder rung that appears, Shea becomes increasingly curious about what lies ahead and feels like chatting, but not about the next enchantment branch. She's mainly concerned about her family back home.

Webster is a natural at reading emotions and inferring corresponding thoughts. If he were a poker player, he'd be able to tell you what two cards you are holding onto. He knows Shea is showing subtle signs of homesickness. Passing time between enchantment branches usually includes some sort of conversation or communication between Shea and Webster. It's a useful distraction to avoid thinking about the painstaking, slow incline up the ladder. Typically, Webster has to poke and prod Shea until he eventually extracts tidbits of information that she wouldn't normally surrender. He is quite talented at that, and decides to put his skill to use once more. Despite his sore feet, Webster is still slightly ahead of Shea and turns around to address her directly, "What's up with you and your brother Christopher?" he asks. "Sources tell me you're jealous of him—that you don't like the fact that he has such a close relationship with your Mother."

Shea's head snaps up and she yells back, "Your sources are wrong!"

Webster tilts his head and furls his little eyebrow "Are they?

I'M NOT AT LIBERTY TO BE JEALOUS

I hear jealousy is a big issue for you with quite a few people back home. It affects your relationships with your friends and drives a wedge between you and your brother. That true?"

Shea looks irritated with Webster for even breathing her brother's name. "You know…what do *you* even know about siblings anyway? You're a *spider*. You hatch out of some gross egg and hundreds of you spin tiny webs and fly away with the wind. I've seen it," says Shea. "You don't know what it's like to live with a brother or sister."

"Oh no?" says Webster. "Well, Miss Smarty Pants, I had a brother once…actually hundreds of brothers. But one brother in particular, our silk lines got tangled when we broke out of our Mother's egg sac and we blew across the sky and landed near a creek bed down in the valley. It was just the two of us. Everyone else was blown away in different directions. We never saw them again." Webster looks off into the night sky, takes a deep breath then continues. "Let me tell you about this brother of mine. Once we settled in, cut our silk lines, and got situated, I took notice right away that he was bigger than me, and stronger than me. His instincts to find shelter and build a web took shape immediately and I felt inferior beside him. I got *jealous*. Even though my brother was helpful and offered to lend a hand in constructing my first web, I didn't like it. I thought he was showing off and showing me up!" Webster stops climbing the ladder and takes a seat on one of the ladder rungs to catch his breath and wipe his brow.

Shea is relieved by the moment to rest and takes a seat on the opposite end of the ladder rung—far enough away that if Webster upsets her again she can pretend like he's not there.

"Truth is, my brother had no ego at all. He offered to help and I viewed it as him bragging about his instinctual abilities. Slowly, as time went on, my jealous tendencies eventually pushed my brother away. He built a new web further down the valley. He visited me less and less. And one day, I woke up at sunset to hunt and my brother was gone." A small teardrop slides down Webster's cheek past his mouth and drips onto the ladder rung below. He stares at the droplet and can still see the reflection of his brother in the mirror-like gloss of the drop. But it isn't his brother. Webster is looking at himself.

Shea scoots closer; trying to see what Webster is staring down at so intently.

"I miss him, Shea," says Webster. "I pushed my brother away with my jealous nature. I guess he could no longer be around someone who, despite his desire to help, was overwhelmed by the ugliness that was my jealousy. And that was it. I lived alone in the valley from that point on. To this day I regret everything about my behavior towards my brother. I should have been a better sibling. It cost me his friendship and I can't get that back."

Shea feels like crawling under a rock to hide from the shame of her comment just moments ago. She reaches into the back pocket of her denim jean shorts and pulls out a ratty, but clean, handkerchief. She extends her arm to Webster and hands him the rag. "I don't want you to cry. Truth be told, Webster, I *am* jealous of my brother. I just don't like talking about it."

"It's not too late for you, you know," says Webster. "Your

brother is still around. Don't push him away like I did mine. Siblings are the most important family members you have. Long after your parents are gone, you know who's going to be left? Your brother." Webster leans in to Shea and rests one of his front legs on her shoulder.

His leg pushes her hair aside tickling her cheek. Fearful of upsetting him again, she gently scratches her face trying not to shrug him away.

Webster doesn't seem to notice and continues speaking. "You have an outstanding support group in your family, Shea. You just need to appreciate it. This jealousy you harbor towards your brother is going to be the driving force that turns everyone away from you. You have the kindest set of grandparents in Johanna, Marie and Lee. Your dad, John, is a good guy. He takes care of you. Your dog, Dillon, is always by your side. And your brother…your brother Christopher watches over you and helps you out whenever he can—even when you don't know he's doing it. Please don't let jealousy break the bond you have with him."

Webster looks up into the tree. The night air is warm. Darkness hugs them like the tight wrap of a grandmother's quilt. Slivers of moonlight cast light upon the top of the acorn ladder. They both see that there is not far to go until they'll be hoisting themselves up onto the eighth enchantment branch. Despite minimal visibility, Webster and Shea move ahead with a newfound burst of energy, knowing the peak of this ladder is near.

"Given the nature of our discussion, where do you think we're going," asks Webster.

Shea responds with confidence. "The Jealousy Branch," she says.

"Ding, ding, ding—we have a winner!" Webster boasts.

As the top of the acorn-adorned ladder comes into full focus, Shea takes immediate notice of the lush green broad leaves that embrace the trunk of the Great Green Tree and its surrounding branch walls. Sprinkled within the broad leaves are clumps of honeysuckle bush.

As soon as Webster sees this, he experiences an immediate sense of home. The honeysuckle is the same as the bush that he had camped out in when he approached Shea in her backyard.

Even in the darkness, Shea can appreciate just how big the leaves are. To her, it feels like they're approaching an enchantment branch built from love. It is already cozy and inviting. And the air smells sweet from the nectar of the honeysuckle. Shea feels welcome.

Beyond a thicket of honeysuckle and broad leaves, a black head atop a brick-red neck pops up from behind one of the budding flowers. "Oh, hello!" says a petite voice. "I'm Liberty!" Her mouth is coated in the sweet, sugary goop that honeysuckle flowers produce. Her black wings are dull and matted with no sheen or gloss. But her demeanor is cheery and bubbly; she seems excited for her nightly feeding.

"You're Webster and Shea. *Am I right*? You're the spider who lives in the Grass Kingdom, and you're the girl who needs lessons in living a better life. *Am I right?*"

Liberty points at Webster and says, "*You* lost your brother

because you were jealous of him." Then she points at Shea, "*You're* gonna lose your brother because *you're* jealous of him— *am I right?*"

Shea leans into Webster and whispers, "This chick is weird."

Webster whispers back, "Sugar rush."

Liberty crawls over the nectar-covered flower she's been feeding on and makes her way over to the traveling companions for a proper introduction.

"You know why the Governing Council named me Liberty?" she says. "It's because I'm a free-spirit. Yup. I grew up without parents—didn't have a name, and here I am, adopted by the Governing Council and brought to this tree. I go by other names too. I'm known as the lovebug, the kissing bug, and the honeymoon fly. I'm suuuuuuuper social, and I'm very forthright. Do you know my vice?"

Webster is about to answer, but Liberty interrupts.

"The same as you!" she points at Webster. "My vice is jealousy! I was an extremely jealous person."

Webster feels like he was just cut off by a car on the expressway. Either that or a fast-talking car salesperson is trying to hand him the keys to a broken down VW Beetle. Webster leans in to Shea and whispers, "This chick is weird."

Shea whispers back, "Sugar rush."

"I heard that!" barks Liberty. She turns her attention to Shea, who, for the most part, has been rather quiet, trying to absorb the whirlwind of words coming from Liberty.

"Well, Shea, I'm wayyyy glad you made it. Goodwin clued

me in that you were coming and I couldn't wait to tell you my story and get you on the right path to a life free of jealousy! It's like carrying a bag of bricks, you know! Once you let it go, you're weightless—the burden of worrying about what others have versus what you have or *don't* is gone!"

Shea and Webster take a seat on a clump of padded broad leaves in the corner of Liberty's great room, awaiting the inevitable tornado of information she's about to throw at them. They brace themselves.

"You know my problem, guys? I'm wayyyy social. The GC brought me in, which I'm thankful for, because *HEY*, I was an orphan! But like, I got here, met all these cool people, made friends, and toured the place—I gotta be familiar with my new digs. *Am I right?* Anyway, the point is, I got way crazy spreading my friendship and love around, because *HEY*, I'm a lovebug! You can change your game, but you can't change your name!"

Webster, ever so slightly, moves his mouth, creating only a tiny gap so that Liberty can't tell he is speaking, and he whispers to Shea, "Does she ever take a breath?"

Liberty continues. "I got to be real good friends with Sydney, the Sphinx Moth. You guys met her, real cool chick down there. Real fast!"

Again, Webster turns to Shea as stealth as possible and mumbles, "Yeah, but not as fast as you talk."

Shea giggles.

Liberty doesn't notice and continues firing sentences out at race car speeds. "The problem with Sydney was that, she, too, is social, because, ya know, she's the messenger, flying around from branch to branch, dropping memos and messages off to other members of the G.G.T. I started getting jealous. Syd was making friends, visiting other branches in her spare time. We weren't hanging like we used to, and I was causing trouble. Soon enough, Sydney was getting annoyed being around me because all I kept asking her was where'd she go, who was she with, and why she needed to visit other friends." Liberty glances back at her flower. "One sec!" she says, hustling back over to the honeysuckle bush to soak up another round of the sweet nectar.

Liberty's energy has made Webster anxious. He bobs his head up and down and taps his feet on the broad leaf, watching Liberty slurp up more hype juice. "Ohhh gosh, not again. No more sugar, please. She couldn't possibly go any faster than she is now—can she? I need a seatbelt," he says.

Shea laughs again and pats him on the shoulder.

Liberty lifts her head from the flower bud, wipes clear sugar drops from her mouth and performs another aeronautical-show-worthy display of speech that comes very near to breaking the sound barrier. The honeysuckle sugar is a turbo booster for her thoughts that neither Shea nor Webster can keep up with. "So that's when the Governing Council—based on Goodwin's recommendation—stepped in and removed me, temporarily, from social gatherings within the Great Green Tree. I couldn't handle the fact that my best, good friend Sydney had *other* friendships. I basically was souring our super cool relationship. And clearly, I was not setting a good example within this awesome place."

Bravely, and cautiously, fearful that *The Hurricane* known as liberty might come at her full-force, Shea raises her hand to ask a question.

"Yes!" Liberty gives Shea a moment to speak while burying her head back into the honeysuckle blossom.

"If you were removed from social gatherings, how did you make your way back into the social scenes? And how'd you end up here at this enchantment branch?"

Liberty's sugar-drop covered face looks impressed by Shea's question. She swallows up another gob of nectar, wipes her mouth, and flutters over to the cluster of broad leaves where Shea and Webster are huddled.

"The GC, girl!" exclaims Liberty. "The Governing Council advised Goodwin to put me through a series of tests where they could see if I could handle situations involving other friendships that didn't include me, particularly other creatures in the tree with distinctly different attributes than myself. Could I accept me for *me* and not get caught up with worrying about everything and *everybody* else."

Shea nods her head as if to indicate that Liberty's explanation is a satisfactory answer.

Liberty continues to address the second part to Shea's question. "That's why they're so cool, girl! The GC. They possess these attributes that I can't quite explain. They just want harmony within the Great Green Tree, and they want harmony in the human world. They want us to be the best we can be. And, like I said, jealousy was my vice! But after I could prove to the GC that I *was* cool, and that I could accept my friends having other friendships, a flickering light went off in my head. Light bulb moment, girl! Soon after, the Governing Council appointed me the head teacher on this enchantment branch of Jealousy. It's my place; it's where I'm supposed to be. So I'm here. You're here. We're here. I'm here for *you*! And I gotta fix you."

Liberty points at Webster again, but this time not to cut him off or interrupt him. This time she points at Webster in a caring way, a way he can get on board with.

"*He* learned the hard way. *I* learned the hard way. You. I don't want *you* to learn the hard way. I'm the lovebug, girl. I want to spread the love, not the jealousy. That ain't the way to be! Don't be jealous of your brother. Love him. Appreciate him. If he's better than you at something, be proud of him. Encourage him. Don't be a hater!"

Webster shakes his head in agreement and seems confident in Liberty's speech. He nods and says, "Right on, Libs!" Then he leans toward Shea and whispers in her ear, "Hey, this chick isn't so weird."

Shea laughs and replies, "Oh sure, now she's singing *your* praises." But Webster is right. Shea leans back into the folds of the broad leaves, absorbing Liberty's rapid-fire advice, and thinks about her relationship with her brother, Christopher. He really has done a lot of good things for her. She wonders what he is doing back at home. Since time is so different here than back at the Stonebrook compound, she wonders if he even misses her. According to Webster, it is still 'dinner time' back at Shea's household.

Liberty chimes in again and offers Shea a gift to remember her time here at the Jealousy enchantment branch. She hands her a friendship bracelet. It is very similar to the bracelet that Liberty gave to Sydney before the fallout, which has since been mended. The bracelet was dipped in some of the honeysuckle nectar that Liberty had been feeding on during their visit. "Have a sniff of the bracelet anytime you feel you're going to slip back into some sort of jealous mindset. Let your nose be the reminder that relationships were meant to be sweet, not sour. The nectar I've provided you on that bracelet will last a lifetime. It's up to you to uphold the lesson you've learned here with me. I can lead the horse to the nectar, but I can't make her drink!"

Shea fastens the bracelet to her left wrist and takes a big whiff of the sweet sugar. Liberty flexes her wings and stretches her tiny arms, indicating that she is way past her bedtime.

Webster pipes up, "Aren't you lovebugs supposed to be asleep at night? You're only active during the day."

Liberty smiles. "Yes, that is true. But if I eat *now*—while the other honeymoon flies are sleeping—they can't get *jealous* of me having a late night snack! Remember, I am a reformed addict of *jealousy*. I never said I was going to give up being a sugar-ninja!"

Shea and Webster rise from the comfort of the green broad leaves and stretch out their arms and legs. Off in the other corner of Liberty's great room, a newly formed magical ladder has appeared. It smells exactly like Shea's bracelet and the honeysuckle bush from which it was born.

"There you go boys and girls…a fresh, new ladder that smells like the sweetest stuff on earth! It's a little treat for you as you climb higher and higher into our Great Green Tree! I know you've been on the move for quite some time, so if you ever feel the need for a pick-me-up, stick your tongue out and soak up some of that nectar! Or simply lick Shea's bracelet. You'll move as fast as I talk!"

Webster leans into Shea and whispers once again, "Ain't that the truth."

"*I heard that!*" says Liberty.

Shea grabs her climbing gear and Webster pulls out his new handkerchief to wipe his glasses clean from all of the debris he had collected on the climb up. They wave goodbye to Liberty, and Shea thanks her for the advice and beautiful bracelet. Shea turns to Webster just before he begins his ascent up the magical ladder to the next enchantment branch. Puzzled, she's been thinking about something Liberty had mentioned a few times without an explanation. And her question is a simple one: "*Who's Goodwin?*"

CHAPTER ELEVEN
S.O.H.O

Fresh from their visit with Liberty on the Jealousy Enchantment Branch, Webster and Shea have a newfound source of energy thanks to the nectar bracelet Liberty so gracefully gifted to Shea. Because of their decreasing energy, it is the best present they could have received. The sugary sweetness of the honeysuckle flower gives quite a boost to the wary travelers. Shea, in particular, is climbing the ladder with purpose.

Webster, with his eight rugged feet, moves swiftly and efficiently. The two are mentally and physically sharp, and for the first time in a long time, Shea and Webster are synchronized climbers.

With a blast of brand new vigor, Shea finds herself more talkative.

This shocks and pleases Webster.

"Webster, I think I need to tell you something," Shea says.

"Do you want to stop here on this rung and take a break?" asks Webster.

"No, I'd rather keep climbing. I think if I stop, I'm going to get too upset and it'll slow us down. I'd rather talk and climb at the same time. I just have to get this out. I don't want to wait until we're at the next enchantment branch," she says.

Webster puts one of his front legs up to his eyebrow, makes a salute gesture and attentively says, "I'm all ears, Captain. Proceed, Ma'am."

Shea begins without hesitation, "I did something bad... like...*really* bad," Shea admits.
"You're making me nervous," Webster replies.

"Yeah, I dunno. I was playing at my friend Peyton's house and I was hanging out in the upstairs loft, but I could hear and see Peyton's Mom in the kitchen below. I overheard her talking about how they were going to buy Peyton a new swing set. The thing is, I have been *begging* my Mom for a new swing set, and then I hear Peyton's getting one!? I was so mad. I walked down the steps towards the living room, which is beside the kitchen. Peyton's mom and dad had gone into the basement I guess to watch TV. Well, I crept into the kitchen and right on the counter top, beside some mail, I saw an envelope with a bunch of cash sticking out."

"Ohh, boy," groans Webster.

"Yeah. You know what I did? I *stole* every bill out of the envelope and I started shredding it with my hands. I didn't just tear the bills in half. No. I ripped them so they couldn't be taped or ever

132

used," Shea snarls.

"How much money *was* it?" asks Webster.

"I really didn't count. I saw $50's, $20's, and there were several $100 dollar bills. It didn't matter. It was all shredded. Peyton's Mom walked in and caught me shredding and ripping," says Shea. "She screamed in horror and threw her hands to her face, cupping her mouth. I thought she was going to smack me." Shea is moving up the tree at a squirrel's pace.

Webster has difficulty keeping up. He is beginning to wonder if the honeysuckle nectar is an energy booster or a *truth serum*. He'd never heard her confess to something so awful.

"Basically," Shea says, "I destroyed Peyton's swing set money. I'm a terrible, horrible, thief," she declares. "By the time I got back home, my Mother wanted nothing to do with me. She sent me to my room for the night, and shortly after, I could hear her weeping."

All Webster can do, besides wipe the sweat from his prickly forehead, is let out a sigh. For the first time within the Great Green Tree, he is at a loss for words. Finally, Webster looks at Shea and says, "We're going to fix you, girl. I'm not going to let you down."

Judging by the muted glow growing from the flanks of the horizon, the cool night air is on the verge of lessening its nip on their ears, necks and noses. Ever so slightly, the silhouette of darkness is being brushed aside by strokes of light. There is no wind tonight, not even a breeze. It is almost as if the air itself was so stunned by Shea's confession that they've fallen dead. Not even nature wants to bear witness to such an alarming admission of guilt.

"I had to tell someone," says Shea. "We're friends, right? I needed to tell *someone*. I had to come clean. Atonement…isn't that what Preston preached?"

Webster cracks a tiny smirk, showing he's a little proud. "It's been slow coming, Shea, but you're learning. You may not see it or recognize it, but you've turned a big corner from when I introduced myself at the honeysuckle bush in your backyard." Webster stares up into the deep blue hues of the remaining darkness and taps the magical ladder with one of his legs.

"Shea, these ladders wouldn't keep appearing if you weren't advancing with your understanding of what this place is all about. Each branch we visit determines whether or not you graduate from it, and *that's* why a new magical ladder appears. It's a grind, but you're getting it."

Moving ahead with increased visibility from the unfolding hands of the horizon's light, the two can see the summit of the nectar ladder. And *that* can only mean one thing: the arrival of the new enchantment branch.

Nearing the top rung of this magical ladder, Shea sinks her pickaxe into the wood a final time before hoisting herself over and up onto the floor of the enchantment branch.

Webster, a bit sluggish, follows close behind. He tugs on the back of Shea's dingy shirt and says, "How. Cool. Is. This?"

It's like a lush, bustling park plopped right in the middle of a metropolitan city. On both sides of the branch floor are benches littered with newspapers. There are several marble birdbaths filled with fresh rainwater. Telephone poles with connective wire line the walls. Stone statues in the shape of various birds, weathered from rain and seasonal climate changes are scattered between the birdbaths and benches. There is even a sidewalk with gobs of gum stuck to it and patches of chewed birdseed strewn about. Had Shea or Webster ever been there, they'd feel like they were only a hop, skip and a jump from Manhattan in New York City.

Shea shuffles her shoulders and wiggles her arms to remove her climbing pack so she can reach inside one of the pockets to retrieve a granola bar. Webster has the same thought. Both are hungry. They sit down on one of the park benches and unwrap their meals. Shea has her granola. Webster has freeze-dried flies. The two look at each other and raise their snacks as if to toast their progress on the strenuous climb. But as soon as they raise their arms, a swooping wind rushes in and something snatches their food!

"It's a bird!" cries Shea.

"Not just *any* bird. *That* is a magpie," says Webster.

"Greetings, human! Hello, Webster! I'm Marina!"

Shea interrupts, "You stole our food!"

"Oh Sorry! Old habit!" replies Marina. "Do you want it back?"

Shea looks grossed out. "No! You ate half of it already. Keep it!" Shea turns to Webster and says, "I think *this* one needs to see Luna The Ladybug and learn some manners!"

Marina smiles at Shea and says, "Nope, not manners. I have to stop *stealing*!"

THE GREAT GREEN TREE AND THE MAGICAL LADDERS

Marina is a petite bird with a tiny black bill and black and white body similar to a penguin. But her white-striped wings have the same midnight-blue accents as her long tail feathers. Her chest is proud, boasting pride and confidence. Her small wings are perfect for swift bursts of speed as demonstrated by the great enchantment-branch heist that poor Shea and Webster just experienced. Marina sports skinny black legs and she hops when she walks. This bird was built for stealth and speed.

Marina flies down from her perch on one of the telephone poles and hops towards Shea and Webster beside the park bench. Dropping the thread and button held in her beak, she says, "I do apologize for taking your food, my friends. That was selfish of me—and rude—and bad—and, well, it was thievery. I'm a master pickpocket, you know," admits Marina. "Before I arrived here at the Great Green Tree, I lived in New York City—the Big Apple! I took up residence in Central Park. It was the coolest place ever. I absolutely loved it—because it was an awesome place for stealing things!"

Shea is still frustrated about losing her snack. She looks at Marina and asks, "So is that why you're here at the Great Green Tree?"

"Unfortunately," says Marina. "Stealing is my vice. Yeah, that is a *huge* problem for me; it's in my nature. I used to hide in the maple trees and wait for people to sit on the stone walls that border the park. As soon as they unwrapped their food—*WOOSH*—I'd nose-dive in and snatch it up!"

Marina flaps her little wings and takes a seat next to Webster on the bench, lies flat on her back and crosses her twig legs. She stares straight up into the tree as if lost in reminiscent reverie then continues her story. "Probably the worst thing I did was steal an old man's wedding ring from a café table. I guess he took it off momentarily so he wouldn't get ketchup or mustard or whatever on it from the sloppy hamburger he was eating. It looked so shiny and nice, I just *had* to have it!" says Marina. "Days later while I was flying around the café I noticed the old man had placed signs all over the park asking for his ring back. He even posted a $500 reward." Marina sighs. "I returned his ring. And I guess it was around that time that someone in the Governing Council got a notion for me to become a member of this big old tree sanctuary. The Governing Council sent a scout to remove me from Central Park and bring me here. Apparently, I had many lessons to learn."

Shea mumbles, "*Serves ya' right,*" under her breath.

"Oh you're one to talk!" snaps Marina, still lying on her back on the park bench. "I heard all about *you*!" She laughs. "I wasn't the one who decided to steal a fistful of cash and tear it to shreds! I'm actually grateful the Governing Council sent for me. I've learned so much about myself since arriving." Marina sits up, looks directly at Shea and says, "Which is more than I can say about *you*!"

Shea rolls her eyes and responds sharply, "Whatever!"

Webster dove into the fray to throw his two cents in, throwing his tired arms in the air like a referee on a playing field. He points at both of them and grumbles, "You two are fighting like sisters!"

Marina tilts her head to the side and shuffles her feet.

"Something like that," she says. Marina then turns her attention towards Shea, smirks, and says, "All I know is, both of us had our beaks in the wrong bark, and it's time to pay the piper." Marina stares at Shea with confident and questioning eyes. "I've paid the piper, Shea, will you? I've been here a long time and even when I first arrived and tried to abide by the rules, I slipped up. I flew down to the Enchantment Branch of the Fire Ants and stole some food from Foster. I intercepted and snatched mail messages from Sydney and the Sphinx Moths; I thought anything with glitter was fair game." Marina hops off the side of the park bench and kicks a pebble across the walkway. She seems embarrassed.

Webster gives her a reassuring nod, encouraging her to continue.

"I even stole sleep from Luna and the Ladybugs by stealthily whooshing by and turning on their lamp lights, making them think it was wake-up time. Of course none of this did me any good," she says. "No...my time of stealing and nonsense was coming to an end. Goodwin had had enough of my pilfering and he put a swift stop to it."

Shea whispers to Webster who has been resting his rear end on a small magpie statue. "There's that 'Goodwin' name again. *Who is that?*"

Webster shrugs the question off and coaxes Marina to continue with her story.

Marina begins a slow stroll, kicking pebbles back and forth while detailing the punishment that had been handed down by

Goodwin. "So I was sent down to visit with the Praying Mantis elders, who, not surprisingly or shockingly, sent me to Beetle Hollow for judgment." She stops pacing and claps her wings together while gazing at Shea and Webster. "You met Preston, right? Righteous fellow, ain't he?"

Shea and Webster shrug. Marina begins pacing again.

"So I'm in Beetle Hollow, right, and the Mantis elders are deciding what my punishment should be for my latest rash of robberies and burglary. They decided that instead of banishing me or removing me from any part of the tree, they are going to introduce a revolutionary new rehabilitation clinic covertly named S.O.H.O."

Shea interrupts Marina and asks, "You mean like the city?"

Marina shakes her right wing back and forth with a twisting motion like a choir instructor and answers, "Well, not quite."

"S.O.H.O. is an acronym that stands for **S**tealing **O**nly **H**urts **O**thers. It's what they named the rehab clinic that reforms those who steal. It's located in the education wing of the enchantment branch." Marina gestures with her head, beckoning the pair to stand.

"Follow me, I'll show you."

Shea and Webster shadow Marina as the trio treks down the sidewalk, following a trail of wild birdseed, which leads to the S.O.H.O. clinic. They make their way past the various bird sculptures and park benches toward a gray, stone-brick structure. Along the roof, on either side of the entrance, are magpie gargoyles; water pours out of their open beaks into birdbaths below. The scene is like something straight out of New York City.

Marina halts her companions and opens her wings directing Webster and Shea to the entrance of S.O.H.O. "Inside you'll find folks just like me…my *flock*. They're getting ready for another class session addressing how stealing affects those around you," says Marina. Her eyes are wide. "Guess who their teacher is," she says sarcastically. She opens the door, and just as Marina had warned, about a dozen or so younger magpie birds are sitting crisscrossed applesauce in a semi-circle on the floor.

At first glance, Shea notices the white board in the front of the room, and on it, repeated about twenty times are the words:

"Stealing is for the birds, and we're not birds, we're magpies!"
"Stealing is for the birds, and we're not birds, we're magpies!"
"Stealing is for the birds, and we're not birds, we're magpies!"
"Stealing is for the birds, and we're not birds, we're magpies!"
"Stealing is for the birds, and we're not birds, we're magpies!"

The space reminds her of her school classroom back home. When someone got in trouble, he or she had to write repetitive sentences on the blackboard. Shea is all too familiar with this form of punishment.

In the corner of the schoolroom, nearest to the closet door, is a video camera mounted to the wall. A blinking red light pulsates every three seconds, showing those in front of it that it is recording.

Marina escorts Shea and Webster further into S.O.H.O. and explains her method of 'punishment'.

"See, here, it's up to me to reform the magpie recruits," she says. They, too, were stealing out in the real world. In case you haven't caught on yet, Shea, that's a no-no. So all the lunch money

141

you took from some of your friends at school, and the money you stole from Peyton's mom and ripped up, well, you'd end up right here in my education wing, being rehabilitated." Marina hops to the front of the room and addresses her flock of rehabilitating trainees in a voice reminiscent of Shea's own schoolteacher, Ms. Brehm.

"Class," she announces. "We have guests. This is Shea Stonebrook and Webster T. Spider. Webster is from the Grass Kingdom."

The class, in unison, makes an *ooooooooh* sound.

"And Shea, she's from the human world."

Whispers, giggling, and soft mumbles echo through the semi-circle of magpies. They are fascinated by the presence of an actual *human* amongst them.

Marina raises a wing and smoothly guides it to her face, making a *"shush"* sound. "Now, class," she says. "Shea is here because she's learning the many valuable lessons of the Great Green Tree, and in particular, she's with us today to learn about the negative effects stealing has on those who are stolen from."

Like a maestro in a symphony, Marina raises both her wings high in the air, pauses then drops her wings to her sides, which prompts her attention-hungry pupils to start chanting a popular phrase.

*"**S**tealing. **O**nly. **H**urts. **O**thers. Sisters, and brothers, fathers, and mothers. This is SOHO and unlike any other, stealing is wrong, we're here to recover."*

Marina leans into Shea and Webster and says in a low voice.

142

"That's our motto."

"Not bad," replies Webster.

Marina turns to Shea with a wide-beak smile, drapes her right wing over Shea's shoulder and guides her out of the S.O.H.O. Rehabilitation Center. Marina, Shea, and Webster slowly walk back down the walkway that led them there. They are making their way towards the central gazebo where Marina first greeted them, passing the familiar park benches, stone statues and birdbaths that line the walkway. Falling behind the slow-paced trio is Webster. Ever so slightly under his breath, he is humming the motto the young magpie birds were just chanting inside the clinic. He thinks it's rather catchy and can't get it out of his mind.

"Before you go, Shea," Marina pipes up. "I want you to promise that on your own time, you're going to memorize the important motto my magpie students recited. As clumsy as it might seem at first, it's going to remind you not to steal from people. I need you to *feather-swear* me that you're going to memorize that and use it should it be needed."

Shea looks confused. "Feather-swear?" she asks.

"Feather-swear," replies Marina. "In your world you use your pinky. Clearly, I don't have that, so it's feather-swear. Grab my wing."

Shea extends her tiny 10-year-old hand and grasps a tuft of feather between her index finger and thumb to shake.

"Understand," Marina says. "The feather-swear is a *royal* enchantment branch promise. The Governing Council will hold you to that."

THE GREAT GREEN TREE AND THE MAGICAL LADDERS

Almost immediately after the feather-swear handshake, a new, freshly forged white magical ladder begins growing from the park floor and continues up high into the Great Green Tree. The rumble from the growth shakes the enchantment branch and buckets of acorns crash through the foliage down onto their heads. Leaves are spiraling down like helicopter blades twirling through the sky. Hundreds of acorns lie at Shea's feet, but not haphazardly. They have formed into the shape of what looks like a word.

Marina flies high up into the air towards her favorite perch to get a better look.

Shea and Webster stay put near the new magical ladder and watch for Marina's reaction.

Marina's sharp magpie vision funnels out the surroundings and zeros in on the gathering of acorns. Much to her suspicion, the fallen acorns did, in fact, create a word. Before calling down to Shea and Webster, Marina pauses, licks her beak and fidgets nervously. Based on the word, she knows where Shea is headed next.

Marina's long, fidgety pause sends a strong indication to Shea and Webster that something is wrong.

Marina is having great difficulty making the decision on whether or not to fill them in on the secret, or let Shea figure it out for herself during the impending ascent. Still hesitant, Marina cups her wings together creating a makeshift bullhorn, and shouts down to her companions below. Her deep bellow echoes throughout the enchantment branch.

CHAPTER TWELVE
ROLAND

"Tolerance? Why would a bushel full of acorns spell out the word tolerance?" Shea is bewildered and looks to Webster. He answers in the most diplomatic way he knows and shrugs his tiny shoulders.

"Really—that's it!? That's all you're gonna do—shrug your shoulders?" says Shea.
Sheepishly, Webster says, "Well, I just dunno." He looks guilty like he's hiding something, but truth be told, he doesn't feel it's his place to fill her in.

Marina thrusts her jittery body off of the twiggy platform and coasts down to the base of the brand new magical ladder where Shea and Webster are set to climb. The two are dressed in their now all-too-familiar hiking gear that they'd grown accustom to over the last nine climbs.

Webster extends one of his front legs as far as it will reach so that he can thank Marina for her time and guidance on the Jealousy Enchantment Branch. Marina accepts the gesture and shakes his leg with conviction. Turning her final attention to Shea, who already has one foot on a ladder rung, and one hand on a hammered pickaxe, Marina whispers to her, *"In order to be tolerant, you must first become part of the solution."*

And with this final piece of advice, the two wipe their glasses clean in preparation for the climb. Webster having his prescription glasses, and Shea, her *Tree See* glasses, they begin their ascent further into the Great Green Tree. They immediately notice that the air is thinner. In fact, the air is so thin that breathing deeply poses a new challenge for the already fatigued duo.

As they push forward up the ladder, the more distance they put between themselves and Marina, means the closer they are to solving the acorn-word riddle that had just appeared on Marina's enchantment branch.

Not only is the acorn riddle giving Shea mental fits, but also, based on what Webster is observing, she looks a bit weathered. Her mind seems stretched to the limit, her body is worn out, and her clothes are dingy and smelly. Shea isn't admitting it, but Webster recognizes that she has hit the point of complete exhaustion.

Shea stops on a ladder rung to allow her lungs to fill with oxygen; the altitude they've reached isn't doing either of them any favors. In fact, Shea squints her tired eyes, peers out of an opening in a cluster of leaves, and swears she sees a cloud. Not a cloud, like up in the sky, but a cloud that is, like, *beside* the tree. She shakes her head from side to side as if trying to awake from a dream, only to find that the wispy cloud is still beside the tree.

"What'cha think, Shea?" says Webster. "Cirrus, Stratus, Cumulus? Stratocumulus?" He is naming types of clouds that exist in both her world and his.

"So that's really a cloud?" asks Shea.

Webby parts the leaves to the side with two of his front legs so that Shea can get a better look at the delicate cloud. "Yep! But it's none of the types I mentioned," says Webster. "Remember, this is a *Great Green Tree*. Magical stuff happens here. Despite you not being the greatest student in the world, surely you know what evaporation is," says Webster. "What you're seeing is the evaporation of the Tub of Tiny Droplets that we visited in Luna's Manor. Do you remember?"

Shea looks amazed. "Oh...yeahhhhhhh!" she says. "It actually smells a little bit like flowers."

Webster tugs Shea's arm and guides her to reach through the leaf thicket to touch the cloud.

"Scoop out a small handful of the fluff and smear it on your face," he urges. "You're *really* going to smell the flowers. You might even feel at peace."

It sounds kind of ridiculous to Shea and her first inkling is to laugh, but she hides her smile, and humors Webster by entertaining his request. She scoops a palm-sized amount of fluff from the floating pillow of mist and splashes it on her face. Almost instantaneously, she is blasted with the scent of fresh-cut flowers. A calm rolls over her as well. *This* is the enchantment of the Great

Green Tree performing its magic for Shea.

Webster even borrows a little for himself by taking his own mini palm scoop. "See, Shea…just when you think you're down, the tree lifts you back up. *It will not let you fail.* Consider that a small gift from Luna!" he says.

Webster and Shea watch as the wispy cloud loses a bit of altitude and descends the Great Green Tree's massive, brown trunk. Webster lets go of the leaf thicket, cutting some of their light source and the path becomes dim again. They also no longer see the cloud. The white ladder that hugs the tree is front and center and becomes their main focus again.

Invigorated, the duo continues their ascent up the ladder towards whatever enchantment branch lies ahead. Shea and Webster are sharing duties as 'pack leader', even though, technically, Webster is the tour guide. The two are moving at a brisk pace with Shea slamming her now dull pickaxe into the white painted wood, and Webster is smoothly scaling the ladder with his eight padded feet. Both are trying to avoid bringing up the mysterious word created by the acorns, because neither knows exactly what to say about it. They each have theories, but neither wants to tackle it.

About three-quarters of the way up the magical ladder, with the top in sight, Webster and Shea begin hearing knocking sounds and the shuffling of leaves. At first, the thuds are random, but as each minute passes, the crashing noises increase in intensity. Every thirty seconds or so, something rushes past them, but they can't figure out what it is. All they can hear is something like wood knocking into wood. It is either a deep clicking or faint hollow sound, depending on where the knock occurs.

"INCOMING!" shouts Webster.

Acorns begin falling at intense pace, ripping holes through the oak leaves and crashing down onto the ladder. Acorns are clinking off of Shea's helmet and ricocheting down the tree. Webster seeks refuge under a ladder rung and waits for the downpour of acorns to stop pummeling them.

A larger, hollow sounding acorn hits the ladder rung and spins off, landing at the base of Shea's climbing boot. Amidst the crashing chaos taking place all around them, Webster manages to scurry towards Shea using the ladder rung's roof as protection from the pounding of acorn shells. Once he reaches Shea, Webster says, "That's a Fortune Acorn. Pick it up! I heard about these things. Crack it open and read what's inside."

Excited as well, Shea grips the side of the ladder with her left hand and smashes the Fortune Acorn open with her right. She reaches inside and pulls out a rolled up piece of thin tree bark with words inscribed on it:

IF YOU CAN BE TOLERANT OF OUR ACORNS WE CAN BE TOLERANT OF YOU.

"We're close," says Webster. "I can feel it...*literally*."

The pace at which the acorns are falling and crashing does not slow down. They are being pelted. Webster and Shea have a decision to make. And Shea has *not* come *this* far to quit now.

They look at each other and nod then step out from under the protection of the ladder rung and begin climbing faster than they ever climbed before. Acorns of varying sizes continue to fall and smack into the limbs of the tree and sometimes into *their* bodies.

Webster squints his eyes to protect them, occasionally glancing up to see how far they have left to go.

"Almost theereee," he cries. "Just. A. Little. Further."

Then, as fast as it had started, the acorn assault stops.

In unison, their hands grasp the top rung of the ladder and they hoist their bodies up and over, landing squarely on their backs. They stare up at the ceiling of the enchantment branch, utterly exhausted from the lightning-quick dash up the ladder. Both are having difficulty catching their breath. And the altitude, once again, isn't helping.

At first glance, the branch seems relatively clean, except for the massive quantity of acorns scattered about. Many of the acorns have holes drilled into them as if a perfectly round straw had dug its way through and sucked out the insides. On the far wall, opposite the entrance ladder, are groves of small Butternut and Shagbark Hickory trees. The trees are unique in that the Butternut is wide and bushy, and the Shagbark is taller and skinnier. The bark of that tree looks like shingles on a roof—each layer of bark overlaps the next. The interior of this enchantment branch is very simple in comparison to some of the other branches in the Great Green Tree.

"Welcome," says a voice that echoes through the branch. "Glad you made it. Sorry about the trouble with the uhh, acorns, but I had to test your tolerance level. It seems you succeeded here, but perhaps, not so much where you're from."

Still lying on their backs, Shea and Webster can see an

enormous, upside-down, shadowy figure walking towards them. With each mysterious step, the shadow grows larger, until both Shea and Webster close their eyes expecting to be stepped on.

"Hey," says a soft, monotone voice, "I'm Arthur."

Web and Shea open their eyes. Standing before them is not the menacing, ferocious giant they had expected, but a pocket-sized, innocent-looking *beetle*...of sorts. They can't quite figure out *what* exactly he is. His shell is the color of sand, and it's wavy or serpentine, like a snake had slithered its way through it. He is covered with a fine layer of hair speckled with tufts of black spots. He has a skinny, tubular beak that reminds Shea of an anteater, and black, oval eyes that look like a pair of tinted swimming goggles that cover most of his face. Arthur's demeanor is that of a quiet, old man who lives down the street, and who's only seen on Sunday's when he walks out to his mailbox to retrieve the newspaper. Maybe he sits on his front porch rocker, counting clouds. He is a soft-spoken, humble creature with a mild temper. And peculiar appearance that almost seems not of this Earth, as if he was jettisoned from an alien vessel then patiently drifted through space for millennia until gliding down to earth.

Sitting up to get a better look at Arthur, Shea asks, "Are you from another planet?"

Webster frantically whispers, "That's rude."

"No, it's okay. I get it—funny beak, big eyes, alien body," says Arthur. "I'm an Acorn Weevil. That guy over there..." he points across the enchantment branch, "that's Bertrand, my cousin and assistant. And yes, we're from this planet. This is my tolerance

branch."

Shea looks at Arthur. "Wait…are you—"

Webster looks sad and drops his head down. He interrupts Shea. "*Roland's* family," he says with despair.

Arthur lets out a sigh and looks over at Bertrand, who had walked over to his cousin to drape his arm around him. "That's us," he says softly.

Shea balances on one knee before finally standing up from the acorn-littered ground. She drags her feet over to a flat stone that's leaning up against the enchantment branch wall. She sits and slumps her body in a position that signals deep remorse.

"What have I done," she says shamefully. "It's the whole reason I'm here. Preston told me that when I was in his enchantment branch." Shea picks her head up long enough to glance at Arthur and Bertrand. "And now here I am, meeting you, having to face what I've done."

"Unfortunately, yes," admits Arthur. "Not to say that the other enchantment branches aren't as important, but The Tolerance Enchantment Branch is a place where one must learn to accept differences in others. One must know that all of us are different. That day in your backyard, you thought Roland was different. I heard what happened. The Sphinx Moths were flying around the tree the day Roland had his encounter with you. They told me. I know you hate bugs and that your friends helped influence you to stomp on Roland because he looked gross. But being *tolerant* of his appearance most certainly would have stopped you from extinguishing his life."

Bertrand joins Arthur next to Shea, who is still slumped on the flat stone. Bertrand has the same basic characteristics as his cousin, Arthur, but he, too, looks different. Bertrand's shell is black and gray like wolf fur. His eyes are rounded, not oval, and he is slightly bigger than Art. But regardless of appearance, they are still family.

"Shea, tolerance is a key component of life," says Bertrand. "There are seven billion humans on the planet, and I can't even begin to tell you how many insects and animals there are. But I can tell you that we're like snowflakes. There's no two of us alike. Even twins. They might look exact, but they're not. They're individuals with exclusive feelings, emotions, and personalities. If everyone in the world treated others like you treated Roland, well then there'd be no more world."

Bertrand hops down from the flat stone, picks up a medium-sized acorn and begins boring a hole with his long hardened snout to extract the nutrients. Webster looks at Bertrand with a confused expression.

"That's how we eat." Arthur shrugs. "You know, Shea— Roland wasn't the only issue when it comes to you not showing tolerance. What about all of the humans—so-called friends of yours that you treat differently based on how they look or appear? Perhaps you don't stomp on them physically, but hurting them emotionally is equally bad."

Shea stays still on the flat stone absorbing everything Arthur and Bertrand are saying. She is in a deep state of regret, overcome by sorrow, guilt and shame. It is the worst she's ever felt in her life. She thinks about the times she made fun of her brother, Christopher, for having chicken pox and looking like a river toad due to all the bumps he had on his back. She remembers poking fun at her neighbor, Sam, because he was in a wheelchair, and the kid in her math class, Patrick, who had giant earlobes. The list goes on. She is reflecting on all of it…all because of Roland. Shea stands up from the flat stone and slowly walks across the enchantment branch floor to the other side of the Great Green Tree. She leans forward and rests her head against one of the Shagbark Hickory's.

"Arthur?" she says.

"Yea?"

"Tell me about Roland. Could you tell me what kind of creature he was?"

Arthur can hear the distress in Shea's voice. He pauses for several seconds trying to compose a worthy description for his deceased family member. He breathes deeply, exhales and tries to memorialize him as best he can. "Roland was gentle. He was sweet. He was always willing to help his fellow members of the Great Green Tree. Some thought he looked intimidating because of his horned head, but all those who knew him knew he wouldn't hurt a fly. I mean literally, he wouldn't hurt a fly. He was a jet-black muscle man with an engine like a hot rod. His motor wouldn't stop. He just kept on going." Arthur pauses again, holding back a few tears. "He was a family man. He volunteered to climb down the Great Green Tree and gather what he could from your backyard to bring back to the branches. He was a noble gatherer."

Shea interrupts Arthur and says, "So the day that I—"

"Yeah," says Arthur. "He was gathering building material down by the base of the tree for the younger acorn weevils that live on our branch. They were going to construct a fort together. He loved the youngsters. But he never came back. That's when the Sphinx Moths showed up with the news we didn't want to believe." A teardrop falls from Arthur's cheek.

Even Webster has trouble keeping all eight of his eyes dry. The entire situation is a sad, ill-fated accident that doesn't have a reset button. Moving forward is going to be the only road to recovery.

Shea's concern for her immediate future becomes heightened when she thinks of Preston and the praying mantises during her visit on the Mercy Branch and the purpose for Beetle Hollow. "Arthur, am I going back to Beetle Hollow?" she asks.

"No," he says calmly. "There's no sense in going back. You've already visited their dwelling and now ours. I have faith that you have truly learned a valuable lesson with the mantises and with us." Arthur turns around and stares intently at a doorway framed in Butternut trees. "That archway leads to the most important purpose of the Tolerance Branch. The weevil youngsters are just beyond that door. Right now, they're learning how to bore into acorns and climb branches of the Shagbark Hickory. They know nothing of indifference. They're innocent, and it's that innocence that we're going to preserve for as long as we can."

He turns back around and addresses Shea. "And you're going to help make that happen, young Shea. You're going to take some of these acorns and you're going to put them in your backpack.

Those acorns will serve as your reminder about being tolerant." Arthur helps Shea unzip her backpack then he throws in a handful of acorns. Some are fresh, and some are already bored into and eaten.

Bertrand finishes eating his acorn then walks over to stand beside Shea along the wall of Shagbark Hickories. "Did you get our Fortune Acorn?" he asks. "Based on some of the bruises and scrapes I see, I'd say you did quite well being tolerant of the acorn battering we sent down. That was our way of testing you. And when you opened our Fortune Acorn, the message inside spoke volumes about how we carry ourselves here."

Arthur hijacks Bertrand's speech. "We expect you'll carry that with you when you depart from this branch—which, by the looks of it, may be very soon."

In the far corner, at the end of the Butternut trees, a pure white ladder stands. It is coated in feathers and looks like a stairway to a place most only see in their dreams.

Arthur and Bertrand stand side-by-side, looking like fraternal twins. Shea stands before them with Webster on her right. The weevil cousins extend their lean legs toward Shea in a handshake gesture, but Shea lunges at them and gives them the warmest, apologetic hug they have ever experienced.

Webster's jaw drops and he mumbles to himself under his breath, "She's hugging them; she's *actually* hugging them."

Shea doesn't want to let go. Her tears won't stop flowing, and her embrace never loosens.

Arthur and Bertrand—two cousins with different appearances,

but one similar heart, speak softly into Shea's ear and tell her, "It's going to be alright, kid. You're doing good."

The trio breaks free from the group hug and walks to the foot of the new, feathered ladder that awaits Shea and Webster.

"See," Webster says. "I told you this is a magical tree. Magic even happens sometimes in the form of a hug." He smiles from ear to ear then reaches into his underbelly pouch to grab his trusty handkerchief to give his glasses a fresh polish before the next ascent into the Great Green Tree.

Shea wipes the rest of the matted tears from her cheeks and affixes her *tree see* glasses. The dynamic climbing duo is ready to roll.

Arthur and Bertrand, with their snouts stretched high in the air, wave tranquilly at Shea and Webster as they begin the trek up the feathery, magical ladder. The higher the two climb, the tinier Art and Bert become, until the only thing Shea recognizes are their round, skinny beaks held high. Suddenly, and without warning, the tree begins to shake violently just as it had done when Shea and Webster were climbing upwards toward Arthur's branch. They stop climbing and nestle under one of the ladder rungs while showers of acorns fall from above. Each time an acorn makes a *clink* or *thud* sound, the pair cover their heads with their arms for protection. Shea remembers all too well how badly the acorns hurt when they strike.

Suddenly, just as before, the pounding acorn rain stops. Several dozen oak leaves spiral down from the branches and drift past Shea and Webster until gently landing below.

Webster peers just past the edge of the ladder rung and looks down at the weevils' enchantment branch. "Well, look at that," says a bewildered Webster. "Have a look, I said!"

Shea peeks over the side of the ladder rung, and sees three words spelled out by the fallen nuts:

WE FORGIVE YOU

The acorn riddle has finally been solved.

CHAPTER THIRTEEN
FORGIVE ME KNOT

Shea feels lighter after seeing the acorn weevils' message of forgiveness. Ever since her arrival in the Great Green Tree, Shea's nerves have been rattled, and the guilt has overwhelmed her ability to think clearly. Like a sack of rocks removed from her shoulders, the burden of blame has been lifted thanks to the message from Arthur and Bertrand below. Her current climb up the magical ladder has been transformed from anxious to untroubled because of their forgiving nature. She wonders if she could be so forgiving if something like that had happened to one of her family members at the hands…*or foot*…of someone else.

The entire visit to the *Tolerance Branch* was a humbling experience for her. And though the weevils showed Shea what the very definition of tolerance is, the one true constant that has been with her during the entire ordeal is her new friend Webster.

It was Webster…the forthright, truth telling, sticky-footed, glasses wearing, nomadic tour guide from the Grass Kingdom. The spider that yearns for a permanent place in the Great Green Tree. He is the moral leader on this journey and the person in charge, steering Shea through this mysterious world of enchantment while helping her to understand its life lessons. It was he.

As they climb the all-too-familiar ladder system, Shea can't help but stare at her eight-legged, fuzzy-skinned travel-mate, looking upon him with thankfulness and respect. Of all the troubled children in the world, she wonders why she was chosen. Why had *she* been picked to explore and learn from this awe-inspiring tree? Prior to being bitten by Webster and shrunken down by the shriveltoxin, the Great Green Tree was *just that,* a tree. Now, high up among the clouds and the sky, it is much more than just a tree. It is her chance at redemption. She realizes she's been given a reset button to go back and make things right. And the entire time, Webster was there, holding the remote control for her.

Webster, though not verbally expressing fatigue, is moving up the magical ladder at a much slower than normal pace. His body language suggests that even he, a nimble, spry spider is hoping for an end to this marathon of a journey.

"How high up are we?" asks Shea. She lifts her chin, looking out past the extension of one of the branches.

"Oh," replies Webster. "We're up there. I wouldn't want to fall from this height, that's for sure." He pauses to use one of his front legs to wipe a few beads of sweat off of his furry, brown brow.

The air around them is thin. Breathing becomes more labored and their climbing has slowed. Neither Shea nor Webster is complaining about keeping up with each other.

"We're in bird land now," says Webster. "Up here, you won't see any more insects or arachnids. There's no fire ants or scorpions living up here. *Up here*, we'll find birds." Webster has to take a quick breath in between sentences because the oxygen is just too hard to find. And once you find it, you want a gigantic, refreshing gulp.

Shea buries her pickaxe into the ladder and digs her spiked shoes into the wood to achieve another hoist upward. "So do you know who we're meeting?" she asks.

Turning around to address her, Webster sucks in his lip, raises his eyebrows and shakes his head up and down. "I actually do," admits Webster. "I know from reading my notes when I was summoned to be your tour guide that once the air turns thin, our final destination is soon to be revealed." Webster cranks his head backward to look straight up into the tree, indicating to Shea that he sees the same pixels of light penetrating through the thick tree leaves as she.

"Look up there, Shea," he says. "You can just about see the top of the *Great Green Tree*. The light is coming through. That's where we need to go, I think. From the looks of it, I'd say we're a branch or two away."

The higher they climb, the more they notice knots appearing all over the trunk of the tree and the neighboring branches. Some appear as loose knots and others appear as tight knots. Both have holes and divots that are blackened and cavernous. Some of the dents resemble battle scars. Yet other knots are smoothly formed with rounded edges. There are no two knots that look alike, and each one possesses its own characteristics, like a personality. As they pass by each knot, it looks as though at any moment something dark and scary is going to pop out and frighten them. The weary travelers have no desire or intention of peering inside any of the knots. They move with caution, their eyes focused on each location that irregular growth or an infection had created an obscurely shaped knot. Webster and Shea prepare for a showdown with uncertainty.

"Webster," says Shea. "I'm glad you're with me. I don't think…Rather, I *know* I couldn't do this alone. I'm really happy you're here."

Webster smiles then creeps past a particularly intimidating knot. "Oh, I like you too, kiddo. There's no place I'd rather be." His eyes dart from side to side just waiting for something to reach out and pull him into one of the oblong indentations of the tree. "Hey, Shea, whatcha say we climb faster and get past all of these, uhh, *things*, and see if we can find ourselves an enchantment branch."

Not a moment later, before Shea can even answer, their pace quickens. The once sluggish Webster, who had trouble lifting his legs just ten minutes ago, has suddenly found vigor and reason to scamper up the ladder. About three steps in the rear, Shea follows close behind. The higher they go, the larger concentration of knots they see. Judging from climbs in the past, whenever there is an increase in tree activity, it usually means they are about to reach the top of the ladder. This climb yields the same result.

"Hey, Shea—just a little more. I think I see the top!" yells Webster. He is clutching his chest gasping for any amount of air willing to camp out in his lungs while he yearns for rest.

Shea is gritting her teeth and looking for that last bit of energy to make a bolt for the top where she can join worn out Webster, who just flung himself over the last ladder rung, disappearing onto the enchantment branch floor above. Shea's curiosity propels her forward.

Shea calls out for Webster. "You over the top?" she yells. "*Hey!* I said are you there? What's it look like? Are there lots of knots?" There is no response from Webster. "Webster! Yo! Stop fooling around. Are there knots? Hey!" she yells again. Still nothing. It is eerily quiet above the last ladder rung. There are no leaves rustling, no words spoken, not even so much as a creaking of the tree can be heard. Shea becomes increasingly nervous about why her good friend is not responding. She digs deep with her pickaxe and scrambles up the remaining rungs of the ladder as fast as possible. Meanwhile, she suspects Webster is hiding behind a branch waiting to scare her.

As Shea pulls herself up over the last ladder rung, she experiences a moment of panic because there is no sign of Webster, only grasslands. No glasses, no handkerchief, nothing is there that would indicate he was ever there at all. He is nowhere to be found. "*Webbbbbbbbbster!*" she calls out. "Hey, enough fooling around, you got me, okay? Nice prank. Now come out!" Tears begin forming in her glassy eyes when she realizes he's not about to jump out from behind a random branch. "Ohh, where *is* he?" she stammers. "How could he just *not* be here? *Webbbbbbbbbbster*!" she calls out again. Shea is now in panic mode.

All that lies ahead are grasslands. Wild grasses of all heights and shapes, beige with shades of burnt orange and brown as far as the eye can see. Tiny mounds of black and tan seeds are scattered about. The more she looks around at her surroundings, the more she realizes the enchantment branch looks like a farm of some sort. Hay bales are stacked, and in the distant background stands a silo, just like one would expect to see on a farm. Next to the silo is a faded red barn with lookout windows and hay strewn about.

Shea thinks maybe Webster decided to look around on his own, maybe venturing into the barn to explore, so that's where she heads. But every time she comes up with a rational reason for why he isn't there, she breaks down crying again fearful of her whereabouts, and that he may be in trouble. She decides to *really* put some diaphragm into her scream.

"*WEBBBBBBBSTERRRRRR!*" she screams. Her lungs ache for oxygen.

"Oh, he's gone, Shea," replies a soft voice from atop the barn window. "Said he had to go, and that you know what you should be doing now."

Shea looks up and sees the creature behind the voice. "Gone? What do you mean, *gone*? He can't leave me here," she mumbles through tears. Shea collapses in the long grass, burying her head into her hands. "Why would he leave me?" she sobs.

"Oh, but dear, it wasn't on purpose. He had to go. It was *his* time. Listen...don't cry. My name's Myra, I'm a Mourning Dove. Some folks call us the Carolina Pigeon. You're at the Forgiveness Enchantment Branch, Sweetheart." Myra takes off from the barn windowsill making a whistling noise with her wings and flies down to Shea's level. Her gray body is sleek with spotted black tail feathers, watermelon-red feet, and a personality fit for a counselor.

Shea can hardly be consoled, though. The thought of losing Webster without even a goodbye is tearing at her tender, 10-year-old heart. "But why? Why did he go?" she weeps.

"Sweetheart, people and creatures come and go. It's just a part of life. Listen, don't be sad." Myra reaches into the folds of her wings and pulls out a piece of umbrella pine bark. There, etched on the flip side of the bark is a tiny message from Webster:

Shea, It was my time to go, but I'm so very proud of you. You've come a long way. I only hope you're willing to go on a little bit further. The magic in the tree only goes as far as the magic in your heart.

Love,
Webster.

"So that's it. He's really gone. Now what do I do?" she says.

Myra looks at her staunchly. "You go on. Look down the tree, Shea. Look at how far you've come. It's a *long* way down, wouldn't you say? All the enchantment branches you visited, all the teachings our tree members have shared with you, and yet here you are, *near the top. That* says something for your character."

Shea stands up. Myra extends a wing and takes her hand. She

guides Shea past some bales of hay and turns the corner past a seed silo to a thicket of umbrella pines. The umbrella pine is the preferred tree for Myra and the mourning doves to rest in.

"Do you know how I got here?" asks Myra. "I once lived in the Carolinas where me and my flock would nest and provide a life for our family and friends. But sport hunting became popular in the region and decimated our population. The Governing Council knew we were in trouble and they took those of us who were left and gave us refuge here inside of the Great Green Tree. It took us a long time to recover from the emotional losses we sustained during the sport hunts. We lost many family members and important friends in our flock, but we succeeded in recuperating and got busy teaching the act of forgiveness."

Shea looks out over the many umbrella pines. Myra's flock takes flight, all making the whistling sound with their wings in unison. Shea is entranced.

Myra looks at Shea and says with a serious tone, "You, too, *need to forgive,*" says Myra.

"Who do I need to forgive?" Replies Shea, looking confused again.

"Yourself," says Myra. "You need to forgive yourself—for Roland, and for your treatment of your parents, your schoolteachers and your friends. You need to make it all okay and forgive yourself. That's the only way you're moving on, both at home, and in this special tree. My enchantment branch is near the top of the Great Green Tree for a reason. Forgiveness is usually the hardest and final step to achieve. You had to climb your way through all of the

168

other aspects of life and these lessons to get to a point where you can finally forgive."

Shea turns away from Myra and the Umbrella Pines to glance behind her, hoping Webster is waiting to surprise her. She is still holding out hope that all of this isn't real, and that he is going to appear and walk beside her like he'd always done.

"Sweetie," Myra says. "Honey…he's really not there. The focus needs to be on you. I'd like to show you something," she says.

The two walk in unison further into the grasslands of the enchantment branch, passing by more hay bales and mounds of black seeds. Shea's eyes are taking in the landscape and she is in awe of the vastness of this particular branch. It is uncanny how much the place looks like a farmer's plot of land. Myra and Shea are hand-in-wing, making their way through a passageway of Umbrella Pines until they reach a tree that stands out compared to the other trees within the Forgiveness Branch. The pine that Myra has led Shea to is twice the size and has twice the girth of the other pines she's seen during their trek through the grasslands. Myra directs Shea to the base of the umbrella pine where a massive knot is centered on the tree. This knot is unlike any knot Shea had seen while coming up the magical ladder. It is large enough to fit multiple people inside. The outer ring of the knot is fat like a car tire. The inside of the knot is a gaping hole filled with blackness and echoes.

Shea is hesitant to get near the monstrosity before her.

"This is the Forgive Me Knot," says Myra. "It's our most

important landmark on the enchantment branch."

"Yeah, but what *is* it? Webster and I saw a whole bunch of these things on our way up the ladder. They look scary. What does it do?" she asks.

"It's a gateway," says Myra.

"Gateway?"

"It takes you to a place. A place you've been before," says Myra. Her beak spreads and she flashes a wry smile. "You *wanna* go in?" she asks.

Shea's posture is slumped. She's nervous and would feel better with Webster's reassurance right about now. She thinks about his note etched on the umbrella pine bark. Is she willing to go on a little *longer*? Is she willing to go in a bit *further*? All of these thoughts cripple Shea. There are just so many uncertainties, all amplified without the guidance and bravery of her now vanished friend, Webster.

She stands up straight and looks at Myra who is standing beside the mysterious black knot. "Webster would do it," Shea says. "I want to go in. But how does it work?"

Myra grabs Shea's jittery hand and takes a step through the opening of the tree knot. "You'll see," says Myra. Neither can see an inch in front of the other. The blackness has swallowed all of the natural light and presented Shea with an extreme leap of faith.

"I'm ready," Shea announces.

Myra leads Shea further into the opening and before Shea can change her mind, the two descend the umbrella pine as if they are in an elevator. Their speed is fast enough that Shea has to grip her belly because it's being tickled. Small holes in the tree allow dots of light to shine through, like mini constellations in a moonless sky, but Shea is having difficulty keeping her bearings. She has no clue where she's going. All that she can think about is the tightness in her stomach and the intense tickle she feels from the drop.

Without warning, their descent has ended. Shea steadies herself, regroups, and stops clutching her belly. "Hey," she says. "I've seen this before. I know what *these* are!"

Directly in front of her, where the exit should be, are groves of broad leaves tangled with vines creating a wall.

"I know this. I uhh, I know what to do! I have to be nice…*I think*…or *courteous*…yeah, courteous, and they'll, they'll move!"

"That's right!" says Myra. "We're at Luna's Manor. Go ahead, make them move then."

Shea takes her arms and flattens out the sides of her shirt, blinks her eyes, clears her throat and prepares to move the wall of broad leaves. Gently, she speaks to the wall. "Could…could you *please* move apart so that we may pass through, please?" An extra please for good measure can't hurt, she thinks.

And right as the rain, the wall of broad leaves slowly begins to separate, spreading apart like curtains. *It had worked!*

Slowly, the opening becomes wider, revealing that Shea and Myra have traveled to Luna's Manor. This is the branch with the green clover walkway, the purple flower blossoms, and of course, where the Tub of Tiny Droplets is located. She is in awe that a scary looking knot could be such a forgiving transport and bring her to a place where she feels so welcome. She remembers everything about her time here with Luna and the Illunalites, and she is thrilled to see the Tub of Tiny Droplets.

"Pretty cool tub, huh, Shea," says Myra. "Luna never told you about how that tub gets filled. Sure, she told you the droplets come from up above, but not *where* or from *whom*.

"No, she di—"

Myra unintentionally interrupts Shea, but continues with her important message. "They come from us, Shea," admits Myra. "Those are our tears that fill the tub. They're forgiveness tears. They're the tears of all the hurt and pain the sport hunters caused us in the Carolinas. But we've forgiven them. And every day we shed them, and they trickle down the tree and find their home at the Tub of Tiny Droplets. Our tears find their way into other branches of the tree as well. We have enough to share with everyone. Our tears are tiny reminders of the power of forgiveness. Everybody here, one way or another, has to take a good soaking in the tub once in a while to remember that forgiveness is as important as breathing."

Shea looks at Myra with a strong sense of what Myra is suggesting.

"Time to take a soak, Shea," Myra says. "Time to forgive yourself, and to forgive your family and friends if you feel they wronged you. Time to free yourself of the unnecessary extra weight resting on your shoulders. Start over. Make it *right* again." Myra gives Shea a little shove towards the tub.

"Okay…okay," says Shea. She continues moving toward the edge of the rock wall that surrounds the tub's crystal clear tear bucket. And *very* gingerly, she creeps in, letting her body slide down the lining until she is submerged. Within seconds, she feels a rush of warmth surround her weightless body, and a sense of calm sweeps over her.

Shea is letting go.

Myra turns around, glancing at the open curtain of broad leaves, and turns back around to find that Shea's eyes are closed and tears are trickling down her cheeks. Myra then looks straight up into the tree as if addressing *someone* or *something*. "I think she's ready," yells Myra before turning back to Shea. "Shea, dear, we must go. It's time."

Shea hesitates to leave the Tub of Tiny Droplets because the power of the water has given her so much relief from the pain and anger she had pent up for so long regarding her behavior toward others. Her moment of clarity has finally arrived. And it is time to go.

Soaking wet, Shea slithers out of the tub and walks slowly to where Myra has been standing, which is a short distance from the entrance to the umbrella pine knot. Myra covers Shea in a blanket of woven green clovers and the two move past the curtain of broad leaves and back into the abyss of the knot. Looking out towards the tub, Myra and Shea watch as the broad leaf curtain slowly closes like a zipper. A few seconds later, the pair are launched back up toward Myra's prairie.

They emerge from the umbrella pine knot cutting a path through the brown grasslands and mounds of black seeds back towards where Shea had first arrived on this branch. Shea gives one last glance over the landscape that had ripped Webster from her, and even back towards the tree knot that had transported her to a place of freedom.

Up ahead, in the main corridor of the enchantment branch, Myra and Shea are able to see the formation of the new magical ladder.

"I'm so proud of you, Shea," says Myra. "You've faced your challenges and you embraced our teachings. Even when adversity struck and you lost your friend, Webster, you stared down that hardship and pushed on. You set your mind *free* is what you did."

Shea doesn't have much to say. She is still recovering from her experience in the Tub of Tiny Droplets and the abrupt disappearance of her only friend. She is dog-tired and lonely, and knows she has another ladder to climb. The new magical ladder stands tall, and is outfitted with twigs and nesting materials. The upcoming climb looks daunting, but Shea throws her backpack on, fits her flashlight helmet, pulls on her spiked boots, and picks up her pickaxe.

"Myra," says Shea. "How many more ladders do I need to climb? I'm worn out. I don't have anything left to give. I miss my friend. I miss my family. I don't have anybody now."

Myra looks up the ladder.

"This is your *last* climb. And unfortunately, this is a climb you have to do alone," says Myra. "We could only bring you so far. It's up to you to finish the magical journey." Myra hands Shea the Umbrella Pine bark note that Webster had left behind.

Carefully, Shea slides the note into the front pocket of her shirt then leans forward and thanks Myra with a hug. Shea then shuffles over to the base of the magical ladder and sinks her pickaxe into the first ladder rung where she begins her *final* climb.

CHAPTER FOURTEEN
THE WISE KING

As Shea Stonebrook begins her solitary climb up the final magical ladder, her attitude towards the Great Green Tree has become one of melancholy and futility. She no longer has her companion and guide, Webster, by her side. She misses her family back home, and she has doubts that she'll ever make it to the top of the ladder to witness what lives up there. In a way, she feels that she was betrayed by the Great Green Tree, and more importantly, by her friend Webster. He told her before they ever set foot on the first ladder rung in the backyard that he was going to be her guide. Various creatures she met along the way inside of the Great Green Tree promised her *they* would show her the way, and prove that changes were going to be made. And here now, she climbs *alone*.

It is still daylight, but the sun is trending downward in a descent towards the horizon. However, it is still strong enough to push streaks of fiery yellow through gaps between the leaves, enough for Shea to see where she is climbing. It is still spring in Shea's world, but the leaves here are changing, like fall back home. There are pigments of browns and oranges speckled within the lush greenery; leaves feel crisper to the touch, much different from the loose, pliable leaves she has experienced up to this point. The air weaving its way through the branches is colder, and when the wind bristles, it carries enough bite to make her wince. Having never been this high up in any tree, she attributes it all to the high altitude. Earlier in her adventure, Webster had even remarked that this is *'bird land'*.

With each thrust of her pickaxe into the soft wood of the magical ladder, the more she wishes she were home in her safe, warm room, watching the moonlight peak through her bedroom curtains. She thinks about her father and wonders if he knows she is gone, even though she's well aware of the time difference that Webster had explained to her on multiple occasions. She drifts in and out of thoughts of her brother, Christopher, and wonders if he'll pull any pranks on her when she returns. She knows how mischievous brothers can be, but she still misses him dearly. She wonders how Grandma Marie and Grampy Lee are doing, and if they are going to prepare their famous meatballs and spaghetti dinner soon. She wants to see Grandma Johanna and sink her teeth into her notoriously delicious spinach dip. And then there is her dog Dillon, who she misses. She hadn't talked about him much to Webster, but he is her furry, *big* brother. She wants to hug him something terrible, but she can't. She is stuck on this ladder, alone, and trying to make her way to this mystical "promised land," she had been told was the *final* destination. And with each rung she passes, her body is screaming for her to stop. Mentally, she is reaching an end and wants nothing more than to go home.

Shea allows herself a short break on one of the ladder rungs because it's so difficult to breathe the oxygen-depleted air. She is so high up in the tree that everything below is a blur. Her body is perched above the ground at such a height that even the clouds are now *below* her, floating near the outer rim of the tree and slinking their way between branches. The way in which the clouds drift make it appear that the trunk of the tree is encased in fog. Wedging herself deep into the corner of the ladder rung, she rests. Peering through a break in the leaves, she watches the lowering of the sun. The yellow roundness of it reminds her of egg yolks crackling on the stove in her house on a bright Sunday morning.

She *misses* her mom.

It amazes her how nature can be such an inspiration for all things that evoke *home*. Maybe moments like these are what some of the creatures she met had been talking about—preaching to her the importance of respect and tolerance, generosity and appreciation for the environment and the living things that occupy it. And that means *her* family too, not just Roland and the Acorn Weevils. She wonders how the egg-yolk sun could be so simplistic yet inspire such an eye-opening epiphany.

It turns out that the power of nature and the magic of the Great Green Tree is very real, and that Shea believes in it.

She cracks her knuckles, stretches her arms and slithers up

the inside wall of the ladder in an attempt to stand up, prepping for the remainder of her climb, though she has no idea how far she has to go. In Shea's mind, she has conceded to the fact that this is the tallest ladder she's had to contend with. She figures the leaders, or whoever is in charge of this tree, can't make it easy for her, and particularly, not on the last ascent. She knows there aren't going to be any favors handed out, so plunging her axe deep into the ladder and moving forward would eventually be her only salvation.

Her hands are chafed, her fingernails have cracks, and parts of her palms are bleeding. The pointy end of her pickaxe is fifty thrusts away from looking like a marble because it had been so worn down. But she presses on, shoving her spiked boots into the ladder and gripping the rungs, making progress at faster speeds the higher she climbs up the tree. Despite having her doubts, moments of sadness, and deep regret, there has been a blaze of determination in her. She thinks back to all of the various pep talks Webster gave her during their epic journey of energy-zapping climbs. She even laughed at some of the things he used to tell her, and it had inspired her to kick out one last gasp of grit and willpower to make it to the top of this darned tree.

The tree begins morphing into yet another landscape. The crisp, stiff, brownish-green foliage that Shea experienced below is transitioning to hemlock leaves adorned with pollen cones. The tree limbs thin and oak leaves generously make way for hemlock. The hemlock leaf is a stark contrast to the oak; its leaves are skinny, pointy and spaced farther apart. The pollen cones that hang beneath the branches remind Shea of ornaments on a Christmas tree. Shea is baffled by how many times this tree has morphed into an otherworldly environment with just a few hoists up the ladder rungs. She has the distinct impression she is finally nearing the top of this magical ladder. She senses that with the change in the leaves comes a change of the guard. Who is up there? She wonders.

Despite the breeze blowing cooler, the temperatures are still mild, but her surroundings have the distinct look of a wintry coniferous forest. All around her, the vegetation is less dense. All she can see are pollen cones and skinny hemlock leaves. Her energy, due in part to the adrenaline rush she experienced when the top of the ladder was within view, catapults her up and into the waiting arms of the last ladder rung. Her hand reaches over the top.

She has finally made it.

Nervous, and with immense hesitation, she peeks her head just above the cross section of the ladder—enough to scan the scenery. She is weary that someone or *some thing* will spy what she is doing as if she weren't supposed to be there. She *knows* she is supposed to be here, but her intuition is telling her not to fling herself over the top as quickly as she had so many times before.

Keeping a low profile just below the top rung, and peering into the enchantment branch, she can see wooden nests like a bird would make, but these particular nests are unlike any bird nest she's ever seen before. The birds she's familiar with back home are robins and finches, and bird sizes of that comparison. These nests are enormous. Each is woven between two sturdy hemlock branches, guarded by a bevy of pollen cones, as if shrouded in wooden armor. If these nests held a bed for her to sleep in, it would have been a California-king. She wonders what a bird that occupies a nest that massive would be like—more importantly, how monstrous is the size of this bird?

Shea begins formulating a plan to heave her body over the final ladder rung then race to a safe nook in one of the nearest trees, but a bold voice interrupts her plan. His baritone soundwaves cut straight to her core.

"Shea," bellows the voice. "Do not cower. Present yourself before me. Step up and step forward."

Shea still cannot see anyone. With extreme apprehension, she reaches her hand over the top of the ladder rung carefully pulling the top half of her body up. She places her other hand on the rung and balances herself to complete the climb. She is now vulnerable and exposed, in full sight of whoever had spoken from within the enchantment branch.

There is a hectic shuffle in the hemlock branches, followed by a *SWOOP* noise resulting in the abrupt appearance of the most captivating bird Shea has ever seen. He lands on a low perch just above her head.

Standing on the branch, the bird puffs his chest out. He is a colossal Great Grey Owl with piercing yellow eyes and a barrel chest. His face is round and rippled like the cross rings of an oak tree. His feathers are thick and marbled in gray, black, and white tufts. His talons are onyx black and curved like pointy samurai swords. His tail is fanned and proud. His voice is powerful, but his very presence *commands* Shea's attention. "*I am Goodwin,*" he announces. "King of the Great Green Tree and overseer of all *hoo*

lives here. I am *hoo* you came to see. I am the teacher for the enchantment branch of wisdom. I'm *hoo* the Governing Council put in charge. I'm the last step. *I'm your way home,"* he continues. "I'm the oldest and wisest inhabitant in this community and an all-knowing creature of habit and discipline. I was chosen even before birth by the Governing Council to lead the Great Green Tree, its inhabitants, and the life lessons it must teach to troublesome children like *you.*"

"Yes, but, how did you—"

Goodwin interrupts. "How *did* I get here?" he finishes. "As a young, light gray owl with thin, scrawny wings, I started as an apprentice under the tutelage of the Governing Council. As I learned to master the life lessons the Great Green Tree had to offer, my wings thickened, turning into a dark, steel gray and my eyes grew sharper. I began to fully understand the complexity and enormity of what I was becoming. Over time, I worked at every enchantment branch in the tree, carefully absorbing the invaluable information taught on each and every branch. I knew that in order for me to *become* king, I had to *become* the role model and mentor to all who came before *and* after. Once I graduated from the program, the Governing Council proclaimed me to be the most masterful creature of ultimate wisdom."

Shea is in awe of Goodwin. She is also extremely intimidated by his introduction and wonders if she is worthy enough to be *sent* home? Has she completed all of the tasks and teachings put in front of her? Has she listened and observed intently on what was being taught? In the eyes of Goodwin, has she done enough to *change*?

"Shea, I've been watching you. I've been receiving reports on your journey up the tree from Sydney and the Sphinx Moths. I know about your *first* step on the ladder all the way until you took the *last* step up the ladder just moments ago," says Goodwin.

His unwavering gaze is stern.

"I know about the *disrespect* towards your parents. I know about your *bad manners* in school. I know about the *bullying* of your friends. I know about the *lies* to your grandparents. I know what you *stole* and I know about your lack of *forgiveness*. I know about your *jealousy* issues and what you did at your friend Peyton's house. I know that you're not *generous* to people and you have no *tolerance* for differences in humans and insects. I know you're not *responsible* at home."

He pauses. "I know that you've *killed* unnecessarily."

Shea's lip quivers.

Goodwin shakes his head with disappointment and takes a breath.

"But I also know *wisdom,*" he says. "I know that you've visited every enchantment branch, just like I did many years ago. You opened your heart to change. I know that you embraced the teachings of each creature you met. I was greeted with the news of every graduation you earned on *every* enchantment branch. Those new magical ladders wouldn't have appeared if you hadn't accepted those teachings. You would not be here with *me* if you hadn't grown as a person."

Shea's eyes are welled up with salt water and drips begin pooling beside her boots. Listening to Goodwin has overwhelmed her and she can't stop the tears from flowing. She has so many questions she feels she should ask, but doesn't know how. She feels guilty about why she's even here to begin with. So many things make her sad now, but she knows she has tried her best to make each situation right again.

"Shea, it's okay to cry. You're here now. You *did* make it," says Goodwin. "You're not the same girl who first stepped foot on *my* ladder so many rungs ago. You're not the girl whose heart was filled with hatred and animosity. You accepted the offer we presented to you and you accomplished the goal—*our* goal. It was *you*," he said.

And through the tears, which are now making quite a mess of her shirt, Shea garbles some words that she is sure Goodwin won't understand through her sobbing. "Yes, but I didn't get here alone," she says. "I had a guide. I had a friend. He was my special, good friend and he's the reason I'm here. And I lost him," she cries, falling to the ground, burying her face in her hands.

Behind her, from somewhere within a thick cluster of hemlock leaves, a familiar voice speaks up.

"But you didn't lose…anybody."

Shea lifts her teary head out of her cupped hands, and through a blurry wall of her tears, she sees *him*.

"WEBSTER!!!" she yelps. Shea trips over her feet while trying to stand then runs full speed into his arms, embracing his furry little body. She can't believe her eyes. "You're here!" she cries. The tears are flowing harder and faster than ever and she can barely get a word out without starting to sob again.

185

Webster embraces her, closes his eight eyes and feels pure joy. "I'm here," Webster smiles. *"I'm here now."*

Goodwin leaps down from his perch. Landing on the ground near Shea and Webster, he extends one of his long wings over the shoulders of the two reunited friends.

"We couldn't make it easy for you, Shea," says Goodwin. "We had to know that you could finish this journey alone. I sent for Webster shortly after you reached Myra's enchantment branch of forgiveness. Part of this journey was about being guided, and the other part of this journey was self-awareness—being able to adapt and overcome a hardship, in this case, losing Webster. You had to recognize the hardships that you put your family through, and you had to realize what happens when you lose someone. Your parents felt like they were losing you."

Slowly, Goodwin blinks his sharp, yellow eyes.

"*You* had to lose someone too," he says.

Webster convinces Shea to release her embrace so that he can brush the hemlock leaves off of himself. Hiding in hemlock leaves awaiting her arrival was a messy endeavor. "So…uhh, yeah," he says smiling. "They sort of kidnapped me." He chuckles. "I felt *really* bad knowing you'd think that I had disappeared for good. But, it was all a part of Goodwin's ultimate plan. And that's why *he's* the king."

Shea is standing beside Webster shaking her head in disbelief that he is *here* and that he is *alive*. She really had no clue where he had gone or what had happened to him. All that she knows is that she can't wipe the smile from her face. Her relief and happiness have hit an all-time high. She knows she was meant to be here.

Now that the fearsome two-some are back together again, Goodwin feels it's time to give Shea a brief tour of his enchantment branch to show her how a "king" lives before their eventual departure. The trio walk down a path of fallen pollen cones then Goodwin marches them down one of the main branches. Just beyond his wooden nest fortress, the branch opens up into a corridor that's outlined in twigs, nesting material, and more pollen cones. It resembles the breezeway of an ancient castle, but is not quite as fancy. Near the end of the breezeway, Goodwin leads them to the most important room of his enchantment branch.

"Before I release both of you from The Great Green Tree, I feel compelled to show you this. This," he says, "is the Wall of Wisdom."

The room is as long as it is wide with a vaulted ceiling of towering trees arching from either side to meet in the middle. Nature's Cathedral, of sorts. The walls are braided hemlock branches, like tightly woven hair. Pollen cones protrude from crevices in the walls as decoration. On the far end of the room is a grand wall with arched double doors and two pollen cone doorknobs. Beside the double doors is a wooden box with the letter "W" on the lid.

"That's the biggest wall I've ever seen," says Shea. "What's behind it?"

"Ohh," says Goodwin. "Lots of *Wisdom.*"

"What about the box?" says Webster?

"That's for *you*," says Goodwin.

"For me?" says a surprised Webster.

Before Webster can inquire more about the box, Shea interrupts as something Goodwin had said earlier finally hits her. "*Wait*—we're *leaving*?" she shrieks. "But I'm not ready to—"

Webster stops her. "*No, Shea*," says Webster. "Our place is not here. I'm to return to the Grass Kingdom, and you are to return to your home. This place...this place was just a glimpse. We're not meant to stay."

Shea tears up again realizing that the end is coming soon and that the very real thought of her leaving this magical place is becoming an irreversible truth.

"What about everyone I met here?" sobs Shea. "Webster, please don't leave me again. *Please* don't go. I'm begging you."

Webster wraps four of his hairy legs around Shea and gives her a big hug to help console her. "Shea, it's going to be alright," says Webster. "Everything is going to be *all right*. I'm so proud of who you have become during our larger-than-life journey. You're not that little girl who gave me a hard time in the yard! You're the *new* you, the Shea everyone's going to love, and the Shea who's going to love everyone back!" Webster grabs her tender face with his front legs. "It's not an end, Shea. It's a *beginning*," he says. Webster manages to calm her down enough for Goodwin to step in and ease the sadness that has come over her.

"Shea," says Goodwin, as he points his feathery arm toward the Wall of Wisdom. "I have a surprise for you just behind that hemlock door. Would you like to see?"

Goodwin is noticeably excited. "*Go ahead...open the door*," he coaxes.

Her heart flutters. With clammy palms, Shea walks to the pollen cone doorknobs, pausing for a quick glance back seeking Webster's approval. With a positive nod from him, she turns the doorknobs and pushes the large doors open.

!!!!!!SURPRISE!!!!!!

It's *them*. It is *all* of them. Every creature Shea had met along the way in the Great Green Tree is waiting behind the doors for her—each wanting their chance to bid a fond farewell. Shea can't believe that The Wall of Wisdom had been containing *all of her new friends*.

Foster the fire ant, and Luna the ladybug is there, both of whom are dancing with excitement. Cypress, the hulking Siafu ant stands next to the hovering Willow the carpenter bee, who has fresh pollen stuck to her legs. The fast flying Sydney the sphinx moth is darting back and forth blowing kisses at Shea. Enzo the emperor scorpion stands at attention with his claw firmly raised at salute. There is Preston the praying mantis, wearing his long, dark robe, looking proud of Shea. Liberty the love bug makes the shape of a heart with her hands and winks at Shea. Flying beside Liberty is Marina the magpie bird, who does air cartwheels, showing her fondness and well wishes. Myra the mourning dove cries tears of joy for how proud she is of Shea's accomplishment in graduating from the tree. Then there is Arthur the acorn weevil. Oh, Arthur. He is holding a picture of Roland, captioned: "You're forgiven."

Shea is overwhelmed by the blissful celebration as she enters the Wall of Wisdom. Everyone joins together for the warmest group hug on the planet.

Goodwin, with Webster by his side, stands back with his arms folded absorbing everything he had orchestrated. "You did well," he says to Webster, giving him a wink.

Webster stands tall with pride.

From inside the Wall of Wisdom, all of the creatures of the Great Green Tree emerge with Shea to surround Webster and Goodwin for what will become Shea's final hoorah with the group. As the laughing, yelling, and jovial discussions begin to quiet down, Shea realizes that the box with the "W" is still sitting on the floor beside the double doors.

"Hey," she says. "The box. That's yours, Webster."

All the creatures stop talking as Goodwin addresses Webster.

"She's right you know," says Goodwin. "That's *your* box. Open it."

Webster looks unsure, but the "W" on the box intrigues him. He and his eight legs scurry towards it. He removes his famous handkerchief—always tucked in his belly, and wipes his glasses clean for the best view. With one furry leg on the outer rim of the box, and the other furry leg planted on the lid, he pries open the box and sees something inside.

It is a branch.

"A branch?" he says.

"*A branch,*" says Goodwin. "Flip it around and read the inscription."

All of the Great Green Tree's creatures, including Shea, lean in towards the box for a glimpse of what Webster is about to read.

Webster follows Goodwin's instruction and flips the branch around.

LEADERSHIP

Goodwin rests his feathered arm on Webster's shoulder.

"Webster, you've done such an outstanding job as lead tour guide here with the handling and guidance of Shea, that word came down from the Governing Council that *you* are to have your *own* enchantment branch here at the Great Green Tree and that it will be named, 'The Leadership Branch,' in your family's honor."

All of the enchantment branch creatures gasp.

Webster can hardly believe the words coming from Goodwin's mouth. "I'm…I'm going to *live* here"? He asks.

Goodwin nods yes, and everyone cheers.

"Hey man!" Foster yells over the commotion. "You're gonna be in the tree, dude! You're *in*!"

All of the inhabitants of the Great Green Tree came over one-by-one and congratulate Webster on this monumental occasion. Each of them pat his back or shake his shoulders as a celebratory taunt. He never moves. He stands still and weeps very quietly, as he joyfully processes the news of his new enchantment branch life. It had been his dream to become a member of the Great Green Tree. All of his life he had lived in the Grass Kingdom feeling he was destined to be a tour guide, never more than a *visitor* of the Great Green Tree.

But now…he's a *resident*.

CHAPTER FIFTEEN
HOME IMPROVEMENTS

It is such a happy time for everyone at the peak of the Great Green Tree. Webster's excitement over being inducted into his new home has filled its brim, much to the delight of Shea, and then spilled over into the hearts of all the current creature inhabitants of the tree. And there stands Goodwin, soaring and proud, basking in the glory of an accomplished mission administered by the Governing Council—liaisons between the animal kingdom and the human world. Their search for a troublesome individual in need of guidance and a fresh new outlook on life led them to Shea. And with the help of all the leaders of each enchantment branch and the wisdom of Goodwin, the task had reached a rewarding conclusion. It is a success story fit for a king.

By now the sun's perpetual glow has surrendered its warm embrace and positioned itself just below the earth's horizon.

Whatever streaks of light remain are now fading into a dim hue of burned orange. Much like when Shea had begun her journey up the first magical ladder, dusk has manifested itself again. The Great Green Tree's appearance has come full circle, which signals Goodwin that it truly is Shea's time to go.

Despite Shea's jovial celebration of Webster's newly administered enchantment branch, and the reemergence of all of her friends from behind the Wall of Wisdom, she is battered and bruised from the expedition up the tree and ready to go home. Deep down her heart makes her want to stay, but her brain knows it is time to return home with Goodwin's blessing.

Foster, Luna, Cypress, Willow, Sydney, Enzo, Preston, Liberty, Marina, Arthur and Myra walk hand-in-hand near the edge of the Great Green Tree, where they form a unity line to bid farewell to Shea. Goodwin, Shea and Webster follow closely behind and station themselves beside a large hemlock branch. Goodwin turns his neck to the left, nodding at his enchantment branch disciples, who are somberly awaiting Shea's departure.

"Shea," says Goodwin. "I'm afraid this is going to be goodbye forever."

"Oh, Shea," says Goodwin. "Words can't fully express the fondness I feel toward you, knowing you accepted our offer of being open to learning such important life lessons. You trusted Webster and took a step into our world, and you succeeded." Goodwin reaches into the folds of his left wing, pulls out a piece of hemlock branch, and hands it to Shea. "This is *your* branch," he says. "I want you to take it with you."

Shea gracefully extends her dirt-covered hand and accepts the gift that Goodwin has presented. On the flip side of the branch is a single word that Shea repeats aloud:

DEDICATION

"You dedicated yourself to a cause and you completed the teachings that *our* Great Green Tree offered," says a prideful Goodwin. "You graduated. We want you to be an honorary member."

"I insist," adds the newest member, Webster.

Shea holds the dedication branch in her two hands and stares at the word that is inscribed on it. The typically less-wordy Shea, has nothing short of the universe on her mind, and she lifts up her misty eyes to address the attentive congregation.

"I never thought I'd be standing in a place like this…in a world like this…talking to creatures like this," she says. "I'm at the top of a giant tree that grows in my backyard, and I'm with the *best* friends a girl could ever ask for."

She looks at Webster with tears in her eyes. "All because I listened to *you*," she says. "You told me to trust you and make the changes I needed to make. You made me see the good I had in me. The story you told me about your brother made me value my family, and made me appreciate the love that they try and give me, but that I'm too stubborn to receive."

Shea turns to all of her friends and addresses them. "You *all* changed me. All of you shared your stories with me and made me see things I couldn't even dream about."

She removes her *Tree See* glasses enough so that she can wipe away the residual tears. She readjusts the glasses and walks to her friends that are making up the unity line. Starting with Foster, she works her way down the line giving each of her new friends a warm hug until she makes it all the way to Myra at the end of the line.

"I love you all," she weeps.

The members of the unity line continue holding hands, lowering their heads in sadness that their pupil, Shea, is going home. They are going to miss her terribly.

Shea moves the fronts of her fingers to the rim of her lips and blows a tearful kiss to everyone in the unity line. She turns to spin around to face the abyss of the hemlock branch, and there, perched beside the edge, stands Webster, with arms wide open. Shea throws herself at him and allows Webster's fuzzy legs to wrap around her like a cocoon. She buries her sobbing face beside his prickly neck and squeezes him like an anaconda.

Neither of them wants to let go.

"I'm going to love you forever," Shea says. "You're my best friend."

"And you're mine," says Webster. "There's a whole new *you* waiting down below. Don't you want to meet *her*?" Webster chuckles. "I'm going to remember you for the rest of my life. *You're* the reason I'm a member of this tree now. I'll *never* forget that. No matter where you go, I'll be watching over you."

Goodwin steps in, knowing he has the unfortunate

responsibility to deliver the message no one wants to hear. Someone has to be the bearer of bad news, though, and as king, it is his duty to convey the heart-breaking words of send-off. "Shea," he says. "I need you to trade your flashlight and backpack for a new backpack. It's a parachute backpack. Once you jump from the tree, you pull the cord, and that will be it."

Shea removes her gear, takes the new backpack from Goodwin, and straps it to her back.

Goodwin then reaches into the right fold of his wing and removes a tiny glass jar with a wooden corked top. It contains a purple liquid. "You need to drink this," he says. "It's the antidote to Webster's shriveltoxin. Once the contents of the jar reach your bloodstream, your body will slowly grow to its normal size. By the time you've floated to the bottom of the tree and into your backyard, you will be full size again. Oh and there's one last thing," Goodwin reluctantly admits. "I'm going to need your *Tree See Glasses.*"

Everyone on the unity line, including Webster, all standing beside the hemlock branch, shake their heads and wipe their teary eyes.

With about as much reluctance as one can have, Shea timidly takes the antidote jar from Goodwin and uncorks the opening. "So this is it?" Her lip quivers. "I...I don't want to, but I...I just...I love you all," she says. She looks at the jar, tilts her head back, and empties the purple liquid into her mouth just as all of the creatures on the unity line briefly close their eyes as a show of denial.

"The glasses," requests Goodwin.

Webster pipes up in a last ditch effort to save the fate of the glasses.

"Can't she keep the glasses, Goodwin? *Please* can't she keep them?" he implores.

"She can't," replies Goodwin. "She just can't. There are rules here, and this is one of them. There's nothing I can do."

Crushed, Webster crawls back to his spot beside the hemlock and looks at Shea with defeat in his eyes. Shea peers through her special *Tree See Glasses* one last time and snaps the clearest mental picture she can of all her new friends, including the biggest one of all, Webster. She scans the unity line, examines Goodwin, and stares at Webster with tears streaming down her cheeks. With her parachute backpack set to go, she nudges herself to the very edge of the tree's hemlock branch, letting the cool breeze glide through her ponytail.

"The Great Green Tree and the Magical Ladders will never forget you, Shea," says Goodwin.

Slowly, Shea removes her *Tree See Glasses* and watches as the images of her creature friends, including Webster, erase from view. The glasses fall to the enchantment branch floor and she can no longer see anyone. There is no reason to stay another second longer. With tears in her eyes and her toes hugging the very last edge of the hemlock branch, Shea falls forward, plummeting back to her yard and letting go of the place she had fallen so in love with.

Immediately, she pulls the ripcord.

As the chute explodes from the backpack and opens into a

full canopy, Shea can feel a tingle make its way from her feet into her legs, up through her hips and into her chest and arms. It is the antidote coursing through her veins, growing her body bigger. She doesn't experience the violent body shakes and sensations she had when Webster bit her, rather, it is a calming awareness that her body is filling out the frame of her 10-year-old former self.

Descending through the dimly lit sky around her, many thoughts race through her mind, which include her mom and dad, her brother, her grandparents, what she is going to tell them and *what*, exactly, they are going to *believe*. She worries about what time it will be when she reaches the bottom, and whether or not her parents have launched a search party for her, or if the cops might have been called. She has trouble believing that time really stood still and that time moves so quickly in the Great Green Tree. Whatever the case, she is about to find out.

The tingling runs up and down her nerve cells as her body is continuing its growth process. Her hands are bigger, her feet grow to normal size and her torso is much longer. She is beginning to feel like herself again, despite her heart aching for her friends in the tree. However, Shea is equally aching for home and the sight and comfort of her parents. All she can remember from just before she met Webster was her dad yelling for her to come in for dinner. She hopes dinner is *still* on the table.

Though it is hard to see because natural light is dimming, Shea can make out the shape of the base of the tree and the toys she left behind in the yard. The butterfly nets and bug containers she had played with earlier that day are still lying where she left them. The house is lit. She can see windows illuminated as beams of artificial light shoot out and across the lawn. From her vantage point, no one is outside. All that she can envision are her parents and her brother, Christopher, wondering where in the heck she is, knowing that her dad has called her for dinner several times.

Landfall.

Shea's feet touch down softly to the ground with the parachute collapsing on top of her. She slips the backpack off of her shoulders, folds the parachute into a crumpled ball and shoves it into the undergrowth of her mom's holly bush—the only place where she can hide it in a pinch.

Once stashed, Shea is excited to run inside and give everyone a hug, but she has one last task. Without hesitation, she skips over to the butterfly jars that have been lying in the grass since her playdate with Genevieve and Josselyn. The butterflies are still flapping wildly inside. "Sorry," she whispers into the air holes in each lid then unscrews the tops, setting the butterflies free. Shea waves farewell as the butterflies happily flit and flutter in the early twilight, eventually disappearing into the nearest branches of the tree.

She brushes off the excess dust that had accumulated on her purple-striped shirt and makes a dash for the back patio door. She flings the door open and is met by a tail waggle and excited sneezes from her beloved dog, Dillon. She kneels down and gives the old boy a gigantic bear hug. Dillon acts as if she has been gone for a week, when in reality, that isn't true.

Shea bolts up the pine staircase and jumps into the kitchen

with both arms extended as if preparing to yell "surprise!" for a birthday party. Her mom, dad and brother have no idea what she is doing.

Shea grabs her Mom and squeezes her like she is a grape about to pop then pulls her dad in with them, so tightly that her Mom gasps to breathe.

"What in the world has gotten into you, Shea?" says her Mom. Her eyes are huge and she can't understand any of Shea's newfound exuberance.

Shea releases her death grip and moves away from her parents, looking at both of them with sincere intent. "Mom, Dad… you guys…I love you so much. I missed you. I'm sorry for everything I ever did. I want to call grandma. Can I call Omi? You think grampy is still awake? I know he falls asleep early. What's for dinner? Oh my gosh, it smells so good."

John and Lucy stare at each other with dumbfounded smiles on their faces trying to figure out why their daughter is acting so off-the-wall. If they didn't know better, they would have thought she came from outer space.

"Did you come from outer space, Shea?" her dad says.

"No. Not space. The tree. I came from the tree." She runs to the French door window and points to it. "That tree," she says. "You see, I was playing out there, right, and well, my friends left, and then this spider was in the honeysuckle bush, and he talked to me…"

Christopher kicks his seat out, rolls his eyes, and leaves the kitchen.

"No, no, really, Chris. Don't leave. I'm telling you. Mom, Dad…so the spider, Webster, he bit me, right. I got shrunken down and I met all these cool creatures that live in *our* tree."

John grabs a soup ladle from the utensil drawer. "Maybe you ought to have some dinner, Shea."

"Mom, there's these fire ants, they taught me about responsibility, and Luna the ladybug, she taught me about good manners. I met a praying mantis named Preston. I killed their friend Roland in the backyard. It caused all of this to happen. There are *all* these creatures. They taught me *everything*. I'm a changed girl, Mom."

Shea grabs her Mom again and hugs her. "I'm different. I'll show you. Call grandma, Omi… call them. Tell them to come over," she says. "Mom, Dad, I just love you guys *sooooo* much. I missed you. I learned so much. I just want to go to school and hug my teacher. I want to hug everyone. I'm going to pay Jill back. I don't know how. I'm only 10, but I'm going to pay her back."

Shea's parents look like a tractor-trailer just barreled through their front door and demolished the house. They don't know who this *new* person is, and what they did with *their* daughter. Shea has become a tornado of weird information and tall tales of talking bugs and a secret tree world. All the Stonebrook's wanted to do was eat some chicken corn soup. Instead, their alien daughter bursts in the room hugging everyone and apologizing for everything she's done.

"You don't have to worry about me anymore," she says. "I learned about bullying and stealing, and what tolerance is. I know

I need to give respect and not be jealous of people. I know about good manners and how to forgive people. I won't lie anymore. And I *will not* kill things unnecessarily."

Shea is talking so fast she can barely breathe, but she has to get it all out. Everything is so fresh in her mind. "Mom, I'm just so, *so* sorry. I'm sorry for hurting you. I'm sorry for being the way I was. I do love you so very much. I love my family. I'm thankful for what you do, and how hard you guys work. I'm grateful to be here. I *truly* am. I know this doesn't make much sense to you, but trust me, I see so clearly now. I know *non*e of it makes sense. But I love you."

Lucy is beside herself. "I'm at a loss for words, Shea. I love you, too. I always have. You're my baby girl, and you always will be. I don't know what you did outside or what alien abducted you, but this is incredible." Lucy is all smiles. "I don't know what you did with my *other* daughter, but I want to keep *this* one!"

Shea and her Mom embrace. It is something that has been missing for such a long time, and now the two of them don't want to let go. Being in her Mom's arms is something that Shea has yearned for, despite all the kicking and scratching of the past. She needs her mother, and her mother needs her. Through the teachings of Roland and his *deat*h, family is what is most important and that is what The Great Green Tree and the Magical Ladders wanted to instill in her. It was a life lesson that had no price tag on it.

After leaving the kitchen table, Christopher had gone to his bedroom to escape his babbling sister. But it wasn't soon after Shea and her Mom's heart-to-heart that Shea found herself knocking on

Christopher's door.

"*Go away*, leave me alone, you crazy person," yells Christopher.

"Chrissy, let me in. I need to talk. Then I'll go away," replies Shea.

With reluctance, Christopher opens his door and allows Shea to come in. He sits at his desk continuing to draw pictures of owls for an art assignment he has at school. Shea puts her arms on his desk and leans into him.

"I just want to tell you that I love you. I know, don't freak out. But it's true. You're my brother, and we have to stick together. I'm a terrible sister...*was* a terrible sister. But I'll show you I'm better."

Christopher continues with his owl drawings.

"I know you don't believe me, but I'll show you. The things I've seen in that tree. Chris, I *really* was up there. Like...*way* high up. I met so many creatures, saw *so* many things."

"Uh huh," he says sarcastically. "Another one of your lies, right, Shea?"

"It's okay," she says. "I understand. I do. But I floated down on a parachute, from way up. By the way... I stashed the parachute behind Mom's holly bush."

"Okaaaay..." says Christopher.

Shea stops leaning on Christopher's desk, stands up, and begins walking backwards towards the bedroom door.

"Well, Chris, just trust me when I tell you it's real. It is all very real. And don't forget...I love you!" she says then shuts the door.

Shea walks down the hallway to her purple-walled bedroom and changes out of her dingy clothes into her pajamas. She can't stop grinning from ear to ear thinking about her adventures in the Great Green Tree. Everything she had experienced is rushing through her mind and rotating to another thought, one after another. It's an endless cycle of memories that she doesn't want to forget.

She makes her way to the bathroom to brush her teeth and ready herself for bed. Although she is still on a mild adrenaline rush, her body is too exhausted to stay up another moment longer. She needs a full night's rest in the worst way. After her teeth are brushed, she runs downstairs and hugs her mom and dad goodnight, and tells them tomorrow is a new day. She runs back upstairs banging on Christopher's door, yelling "Goodnight, Chris!" Shea turns off the light switch and falls into her bed with a thud that could have been heard two blocks away.

The day is finally *over*.

Morning arrives with the glorious sun sending beams of salutations through Shea's window. The old Shea would have barked something mean, and slammed her curtains shut. The new Shea opens both of her eyes and stares out of the window with a hopeful smile that the day will bring enchantment.

"Today's my new beginning," she says to herself.
Walking down the hallway to the stairwell, Shea can smell some of mama's best eggs and bacon cooking on the stove. She immediately thinks about that egg yolk, and how the roundness of the sun way up on Goodwin's branch had made her think of *home*.

Dad is at the table, Mom is by the stove, and Chris…well, Chris isn't there. At the bottom of the steps, Shea looks at her parents and says, "Good morning, guys! Mmmm, it smells so good, Mom. Dad, what cha' reading? What a great day, today, huh?"

Suddenly, a faint tap on the kitchen window catches Shea's attention. When she looks, no one is there. The tap occurs again. This time, she sees something.

It is Christopher. He signals her with his index finger to go to the French doors in the dining room.

She opens the door and asks him why he is sneaking around the window.

"Shea, there's a parachute by the side of the house!" he squeals.

"Yes I know, Chris," she replies. "I put it there, remember?"

"Are you saying you were up in that tree? You *really* were up there? How did you…but when you…what creatures did you see again? I mean, you said, I said, you said, I mean, I didn't believe you. You burst into my room, tell me you love me…*weird*… and then go on about you being way up in our tree—parachuting down. Who's going to *believe* something like that? Show me these creatures, Shea. I want to *see* them."

"Can't, silly," she says. Shea giggles and pats Christopher on the shoulder.

It was November and six months had gone by since Shea's adventure in the Great Green Tree. Life at the Stonebrook's was better than ever. Shea was excelling in school. She joined the math team and was playing soccer in her spare time. Her friends would visit frequently after school to have play dates. The family would gather once a week for a grampy and grandma spaghetti and meatballs dinners with Omi Johanna bringing her world famous spinach dip as an appetizer.

The family embarked on many weekend getaway trips, focusing their attention on "we" time. Shea even did more chores in the house earning an honest wage from her dad so that she could start to pay back Jill for the money she ripped apart. Paying Jill back was going to take a long time, but Shea had to start somewhere.

The house was a house of harmony, no longer a place of disdain and agony. Shea wanted to be home to help around the house, playing with her brother, and to ask neighbors if they needed any assistance with anything. Her home became her little sanctuary and she was proud to live there.

However, despite her turning a new leaf, and generally enjoying her new life, she always had a place in her heart for sadness—sad that she no longer could see her tree friends—sad that she couldn't talk with Webster or receive his sound advice on important life lessons. Often times she'd sit on the deck steps by the back door patio, see a carpenter bee flying around, and wonder if that was Willow collecting pollen for her enchantment branch. When she rode her bike, she'd see fire ants marching erratically on the sidewalk carrying bits of old food and leaves. She wondered if they were Foster and his crew of workers fulfilling an order for Queen Felonia and the anthill. There were times she'd retrieve the mail from the mailbox and see a ladybug walking along the post, spread its tiny wings and fly away. She thought maybe that was Luna dropping by to say hello.

There was no way of telling for sure. She just knew in her heart that there was a hole. All that she could do to fill that hole was hope that the creatures she saw *were* her friends, and to uphold the promise she made to them by sustaining her good behavior and *"beeing"* the new Shea that they all had hoped for.

And she most certainly was accomplishing that, even despite the fact she missed all her tree friends dearly.

Winter was soon around the corner for the Stonebrook's, and through her bedroom window, Shea could see that all of the leaves of the trees had begun to fall. The "Great Green Tree" with which she was so familiar, was starting to thin out and change color. The leaves were still present and hugged the oak branches that jutted out from the massive trunk, but Shea could see the gaps. The leaves were still somewhat green, but clearly, the tree was changing. She had days where she was devastated that she'd never see her creature friends again, and today happens to be one of those days.

Shea mopes from room to room thinking about her dear friend Webster and what he might say to her on a day like this to help boost her spirits. She thinks of the Tub of Tiny Droplets and how a soothing soak in that tub would pry her sadness away. She thinks of the Forgive Me Knot on Myra's branch and the beauty of Beetle Hollow. She thinks maybe a cold splash of water from the bathroom sink would energize her and shake her out of the depressive funk that she's found herself in. So she heads towards the upstairs bathroom.

After turning the water to cold, filling her palms and splashing her face, she grabs the towel hanging from the ring on the wall beside the window. She dries her face and opens her closed eyes within the towel peering down at the yard below. It is then that she catches a glimpse of something at the base of the tree. View of the object is partially obstructed by leaves swaying in the wind. She throws the towel down on the countertop and runs downstairs, almost tripping over her feet to get to the back patio door.

There—by the foot of the tree she sees it. Her eyes had not been fooling. There *is* an object there. It had *not* been a figment of her imagination. She stands by the back patio French doors and gazes at the item she had seen from the window.

It is a box.

Without her shoes and socks on, Shea opens the French doors and walks ever so slowly to the small, wooden box sitting at the base of the tree. It is eerily similar to the box that Webster had received on Goodwin's branch. She leans forward and notices there is an "S" etched on the lid.

"S" for Shea? She wonders.

She looks around to see if anyone is watching her or if her brother or parents are nearby, thinking that maybe they had seen the mysterious box as well. But she can see no one. It is just the box and she. With nervous anticipation, Shea carefully pries open the box with her skinny fingers until the sun's light shines in on its contents.

There is a folded piece of bark from the umbrella pine found at Myra's enchantment branch sitting on top of an obscure item blanketed in purple cloth. Shea reaches inside the box, removes the umbrella pine note and unfolds it.

Shea, you've upheld your promise to us on turning a new leaf. You have accepted the "Dedication" branch and have continued to master ALL of the teachings the Great Green Tree has offered you. As a token of appreciation from the Governing Council, it is with great joy and honor on my behalf to present this gift to you.

Shea sets the note aside and begins to unwrap the soft, purple cloth that shrouds the obscure object. She starts to quietly weep.

It is a full-sized pair of *Tree See Glasses*!

Shea cries, clutching the glasses to her heart, while she continues to read the rest of the umbrella pine note that was left for her.

From this day forward, these glasses will grant you sight into the Great Green Tree. Your dedication to change gives you access anytime your heart desires. We'll "see" you soon. Yours forever,

-W

Shea doesn't hesitate. She puts the glasses on, looks up the tree, and…

CREATURE FEATURE

Ah, you found us! Did you use the Table Of Contents or did you just keep reading? What did you think of the book? Did you like it? Did you come to the CREATURE FEATURE because you want to learn more about each enchantment branch's leader? I'll wait for your answer...

Okay, good.

Below, you'll find a SUPER SECRET password that only YOU will know. In order to enter the CREATURE FEATURE website, you'll need to use the way cool password at the way cool website. What's the website all about you ask?

Keep reading...

Find out where the Great Green Tree's creatures are from, and what their habitats are like. Get to know the leaders of the Great Green Tree! Here's what you do...

Go to
www.GREATGREENTREE.com
and type in this SUPER SECRET password

Now go! Discover their history!

The original "Great Green Tree" that grows in my backyard.

ACKNOWLEDGEMENTS

Tony Maulfair—for your rock solid illustrations. We have a good thing going. I appreciate you. The books wouldn't be the same without your artistic contributions.

Vanessa Gonzales—my editor. Thank you for your insights, vision, and knowledge. You are awesome. And you are one amazing writer. More people need to know about you. Please visit Vanessa at vanessagonzales.com

Mary Grace Corpus—for your fantastic illustration contributions. Please visit Mary Grace at marygracecorpus.com

Dean Montgomery and 1218 Artist—for your front cover art assistance. Dean, your memory will live forever through this book. Thanks for your friendship. I'll miss you.

Aubrey and Cameron—for providing constant inspiration. You two are the reasons behind my writing.

Melisa—for the journey we've been on for so long. Thanks for always being beside me.

Special thanks to: Katja (my Mom), Don and Michelle Smith, Todd Shill, David Snively, Roy Combs, Ryan Savino, Josh Witman, Jaci Moos, Floyd Stokes, Vladimir Winecoor, Cody Jones, Jay Mohr, The Mohriorrs, my friends and family, and kids who love reading. You have all contributed in your own unique way.

Thank you to everyone who has supported me. I hope you found some magic within these pages, and in your own life.

#WE

ALSO BY STEPHEN KOZAN

FOR SCHOOL SPEAKING ENGAGEMENTS
Contact: readyaimwrite@gmail.com or 717.903.9393

Facebook.com/authorstephenkozan

Twitter.com/stephenkozan

To leave a Goodreads review for the book,
please visit Goodreads.com and type The Great Green Tree And
The Magical Ladders in the search bar.

ABOUT THE AUTHOR

Stephen grew up around Harrisburg, Pennsylvania, in a small town called Bressler. From an early age, he enjoyed writing and creating stories. His passion for writing started with poetry in grade school, followed by writing music lyrics and short stories in high school. Post graduation, he attended Harrisburg Area Community College, studying literature, and creative writing courses. In addition to publishing *The Great Green Tree And The Magical Ladders,* Stephen also wrote and published the fiction book, *The Journal Of A Lifetime*, which can be found online and in bookstores. He lives in the Harrisburg area with his wife, two children, and dog, Dillon. He can be found online at: StephenKozan.com